Spiderweb Alley

Book One
of
THE ELVERIE ROAD

Spiderweb Alley

by
Verlyn Flieger

The
Gabbro Head

Wayzata, Minnesota
2024

Cover art features and Post-Piece:
Copyright © 2024 by Mia Palladino

Cover background art and cover design:
Copyright © 2024 by Semnitz™

ISBN: 978-1-7325799-6-5

Printed in the United States of America.

The Gabbro Head Press LLC

Email: editorial@gabbrohead.com
U.S. Mail: P.O. Box 53, Wayzata, Minnesota 55391

www.gabbrohead.com

Also by Verlyn Flieger:

<u>Literary Criticism</u>

Splintered Light:
Logos and Language in Tolkien's World

A Question of Time:
J. R. R. Tolkien's Road to Faërie

Interrupted Music:
the Making of Tolkien's Mythology

Green Suns and Faerie: Essays on J. R. R. Tolkien

There Would Always Be a Fairy Tale:
More Essays on Tolkien

<u>Fiction</u>

Arthurian Voices

A Waiter Made of Glass: Stories and Poems

Acknowledgements

I would like to acknowledge and thank Sibbie O'Sullivan, Sarah Pleydell, Cindy Matsakis and Linden von Eichel: ladies, your encouragement, blunt criticism, and stringent opinions made me want always to do better.

— Verlyn Flieger
May 2024

This book is dedicated to

Vaughn Howland

who met me every morning
with a typescript scribbled with red ink
and gave me reason to re-write.

Elverie, noun. obscure.
Fairyland, Elfland, the Otherworld of myth and folktale. Often conflated with the Land of the Dead. Dialect term from the west country still in use in remote areas of the coast.

— "Glossary" in *Stories That Tell Themselves*, by M. McKennan, TopTree Press, 2007.

These things happened in a place
where no one goes anymore,
a nameless country of steep cliffs
and icy rivers, and dark forests
where strange beasts prowl unchecked.

Cottages of grey stone perch on headlands by the sea.
Along the coast fishing-boats beach on rocky shingle
where fishermen unload their catch.
Over it all a water-color sky is filled
by day with clouds like drifting sails,
and at night with the curious patterns of stars.
That is in summer.

In winter, grey roofs the earth.
Sometimes a north wind comes,
and the ground covers with white,
rivers lock with ice and trees glaze and glitter
under a cold sun.

Then the people bank the snow high
around their houses to baffle the wind.
They bar the shutters to keep out the night,
and draw close to their fires.

They tell the stories that folk tell
on winter nights.
The tale of Kath and Mick
is one of these stories.

On the Road

It was a fine evening, cool but not cold, with a steady onshore breeze. On the seaward side of the road, separated from it only by a narrow belt of windbent trees, cliffs dropped sheer to the waves that beat against them.

On the landward side hillsides reared like the shoulders of giants half buried in the earth. There was no traffic, and the road soared and dipped with the rise and fall of the land. Mick, at the wheel, concentrated on negotiating the switchbacks. Kath drank in the scenery.

For a while they drove in silence through the slow, luminous northern twilight. Mick had met Kath at the coach station and immediately, as she had mock-complained, "hustled her off to parts unknown."

Unknown but beautiful, she reflected, enchanted by the slow-dying sunset and the way it lighted earth and sky.

Mick spoke. "What are you thinking?"

"That we're in a different world from where you picked me up in — what's its name? That little town?"

"Great Wicken."

"Some 'great'! Is there a Little Wicken that's even smaller?"

"Probably. Somewhere. Out in the boonies."

"I almost hope not. It's so remote up here. Kind of uncanny—can you feel it? Like fairyland. Maybe it's the light. Or the stillness. I can hardly even hear the waves."

"You'll hear them where the road gets closer to the water, but I agree about the light. It is spooky."

"Yes, but I like that."

You would, he thought. *Anything out of the ordinary is right up your alley.* He glanced affectionately at her profile silhouetted against the light. Memory swept him back.

> *The Information Desk in Special Collections. The scent of freesias in a jam jar next to the computer competed with the library smell of old paper and rubbed bindings. The redhead behind the computer was new, probably a student assistant, probably responsible for the freesias. Her oversize hornrims gave her green eyes a nearsighted innocence, and the dusting of freckles on her nose made her look even more like a kid. Her smile reminded him of the Cheshire Cat.*
>
> *"Can I help you?"*
>
> *"I hope so. I'm looking for a book."*
>
> *"You've come to the right place. Any old book? Or a particular book?"*
>
> *Oh ho. Ms. Hornrims had a bite that belied her innocent look.* "Yes. A particular book. Popular Antiquities, *by Auberon Layland, two volumes, published in 1886. In 'particular' (he gave her back her sarcasm) Volume II."*
>
> *She shook her head. "Never heard of it."*

He relented. "You're not alone. Neither have most people. It's hard to find. Which is why I'm here. Your online catalogue says you have it, but I can't find it. It's not checked out, but it's not on the shelf."

Her fingers danced over the keyboard, hesitated, danced again. She peered at the monitor. "We have it all right. Both volumes. But they're 'Out to Repairs.' That means in the basement, in the shop. Probably be re-shelved by the end of the month. You can put in a green slip for the volume you want and we'll let you know when it's ready."

"No, I need it now. End of the month is too late."

"Sorry. If you could come back in a week . . ."

"Not possible. I've got to hand in my thesis the end of this week. I absolutely must check some references and verify a couple of footnote citations."

"You're writing a thesis on antiques?" She seemed surprised.

"Not antiques. Antiquities. Folklore, fairy tales, local customs, superstitions."

"Oh, fairy tales."

She brightened, but before she could go on he added, "I've only got the one day free, and I've spent

4

half of it just trying to chase down the book. Please don't say the other half's going to be a loss too."

She tilted her head to one side, considering, the feathery bangs spilling untidily into her eyes.

Time to pull out the stops. "Look, Miss . . . um – "

"Kath," she said.

"Good to meet you, Kath. My name's Mick." Out came all the stops. "Look, Kath, you're my only hope. There's not another library within traveling distance that has that book. What will it take? Can I buy you a coffee? Mocha? Hazelnut? Chocolate? Whipped cream? The sky's the limit."

"Well, when you put it that way. . . ."

The wide, generous smile that lit up her face made her suddenly pretty, and her next words were music.

"Okay, big spender. I have a buddy in Repairs. Here's a green slip. Fill out the call number and I'll phone it down. You should get both volumes in about half an hour. Do you have a study carrel?"

"No, but I'll get one."

She shook her head. "No you won't. They're all in use. It's the week before exams."

5

"Yes, I know. For me too, and I should be hard at work thinking up unanswerable questions for my students. Isn't there a corner somewhere that nobody else wants? I'll take anything you've got."

"How about a study table on rollers? There's a spare one there next to the elevators. Wheel it over, and I'll scrounge you up a chair."

"You're a lifesaver. Coffee coming up."

"Save it for my break. Cappuccino, hazelnut and two sugars."

The study table was a rickety little number whose plastic wheels rattled the library silence when he manhandled it over to the Information Desk. She scrounged a chair and he sat and waited. When the half-hour mark had come and gone, he went to check.

"They can't find it," she told him. "I just called down again, and they'll keep looking. How about I take you up on that coffee, and when we come back it'll be here."

"Fair enough."

He made good on the cappuccino, hazelnut and two sugars. He had a double espresso. They spent her break curled around the coffee cartons in the courtyard where he apologized for breaking the quiet of the reading room.

6

"Although," he said, "if they were minding their own business, keeping their noses in their books, they wouldn't have noticed."

"Oh come off it. Nobody minds their own business all the time. That's one of the Seven Deadly Virtues."

He was charmed. "What are the other six?"

"Let's see." She ticked them off on her fingers. "Not Stepping on the Cracks, Not Coloring Outside the Lines, Looking Before you Leap, Being on Time, Saving for a Rainy Day, and ummm . . . Going Without Dessert."

"Ah, that's where I'd fall into Error," he confided. "Never could pass up forbidden fruit."

"The only kind worth eating," she agreed.

He told her about his thesis and the collecting trip he was planning once exams were over. She asked him about Popular Antiquities and whether "customs and sayings" included fairy tales. Her love of fairy tales marched in step with his own studies, except that with her the tales weren't studied: they were lived.

"Relic of my misspent childhood," she confessed. "While the other kids were trading rock star photographs, I was turning round and round with Baba Yaga in the hut on chicken legs. Chicken legs! I mean — really! What a concept!"

"You were in the right place," he assured her. "Rock stars come and go, but chicken legs will never let you down."

There came a sideways quirk of the head and a look from under the bangs.

"I wouldn't bet on that," she countered. "Sometimes fairy tales don't live up to expectations."

"Hold on a minute," he said. "The whole point of a fairy tale is to live up to expectations. The Happy Ending, remember?"

"Yes, but how you get to the Happy Ending is important. And some stories use pretty weird devices. Like 'The Frog Prince.' I hated that one when I was a kid. I wanted to re-write it. Still do. It's all wrong. Why would slamming the poor frog against the wall turn him into a prince? It never did that for me. The princess is a spoiled little twit who makes a promise she doesn't intend to keep, and uses violence to get out of the bargain. A real brat, she was. Talk about expectations. I'll bet you anything they didn't live happily ever after."

"Possibly not," he conceded. She wasn't as naive as she looked, and besides, he was enjoying the

8

argument. "It's the flip side of *Beauty and the Beast*, where compassion brings about metamorphosis. 'The Frog Prince' – the proper title is 'Iron Henry' for reasons I never could fathom – is the reverse of the medal. But isn't the mismatch the whole point? A princess and a frog: that isn't supposed to be a match made in heaven."

"I've seen worse," she said. "That frog just needed the right princess. He obviously deserved somebody better. Like me."

She was talking, Mick noticed with amusement, as if the story had happened just yesterday, and she had read it in a gossip magazine. It was the first of many times he was to come up against her penchant for making herself a part of the story, as if she recognized no distinction between fiction and real life.

Popular Antiquities *never did show up, but by then he didn't care. He was more than charmed. He was in love.*

He was still in love when Kath's voice broke his reverie. "I hope where we're going isn't too uncann—. . . Mick, look out!"

9

He slammed on the brakes and the car slewed off the road, narrowly missing trees and coming to a hard stop inches from the cliff edge.

For a long breath neither spoke. Mick was first.

"What the hell was that about?"

"A dog ran in front of the car. Didn't you see it?"

"No."

"A little red and white dog, a hound or beagle or something."

"I did not see any dog. But do you see where we are? Another inch and we'd have been over the edge."

He re-started the car, backed with care away from the precipice, and onto the road and so away. They were both shaken and silent: Mick with his eyes on the road, Kath worrying what to say. At last she put a hand on his arm.

"Mick, I'm sorry. I didn't mean to spook you. But you darn near hit him."

"Better him than us."

"Better nobody. *Pax*?"

"Of course *pax*. But don't do that when I'm driving. Or at least give me some warning."

"Where do you think he came from? The dog. I don't see any houses."

"Not along the road." He concentrated on a hairpin turn. "Houses around here are mostly down in the coves or up on the tops. Few and far between in any case. Not what you'd call a settled part of the world."

She shivered.

"You okay?"

She nodded. "I'm fine."

Was she? She didn't seem it, thinner than he remembered, smooth skin stretched tight across the cheekbones. The usual wisps of hair were falling into her eyes, and the hollows under them made her look paler than he liked.

"You don't look all that great."

She jabbed back. "You're not so hot yourself, mister. Better keep your eyes on the road. You didn't see that dog, and now there's mist."

He saw that she was right. While they talked, tendrils of mist were snaking across the road, thickening by the minute.

"Mick, can you slow down a little? Between the fog and the switchbacks this road

11

is an accident waiting to happen. How many twists and turns does it have, anyway?"

He cut his speed and switched on the headlights. "Almost as many as you do. I thought you'd enjoy the scenic route. The locals call it Cliff Road. I call it Spiderweb Alley."

"Why on earth?"

"You know those draglines spiders hang between trees? You can walk into them before you know it. Like this mist we're driving through."

"Should we have taken the motorway?"

"The motorway doesn't go where we're going."

"Where are we going? How far is this place?"

"As the crow flies, about fifteen minutes. But as the road goes, at least half an hour."

"That crow gets around. What's a crow doing up here anyway? I was expecting seagulls."

"Nothing up here is what you'd expect."

"No, not even you. What's got into you? You're as jumpy as a pig on ice."

"Not what's got into me, but what I've got into." Mick put his arm across the back of the seat.

Kath could feel his excitement, barely contained.

"There's a gab tonight by a local storyteller, somebody I've never heard of. We've been invited."

"What's a *gab*?"

"A story-telling evening. In the local dialect gab means '*the place where stories are real*.' There's a chance I'll be the first to hear them."

"You sound like a big game hunter. Bring 'em back alive."

"Well this may be game no one else has hunted. I could be the first outsider to hear."

"But you didn't bring a tape recorder, not even a pencil. Unless you've got wires stuck to your chest like a spy movie."

"None of the above. The locals are suspicious of outsiders. A few years ago developers were trying to buy land. Accidents happened; the survey marks disappeared; there were even hauntings, strange noises, things

13

going bump in the night. They got the message and left."

The mist was thickening by the moment, snagging in the trees and curling around the car, bringing with it a damp chill. Kath shivered and hugged her arms. When Mick pulled off his sweater, she wrapped it around herself snugly.

"Hunting or haunting—take your pick."

"I hope neither. We're not developers. But we are outsiders. So we mind our manners."

"Ah, I see. Don't spook the horses."

"Don't what?"

"My dad used to say, 'Do what you want, just don't do it in the street and spook the horses.'"

"Your dad's right. And the horses hereabouts are skittish. These gabs, they're hard to break into. So we mind our manners. No asking questions."

"Can I ask you questions?"

"If you ask them before we get there."

"Okay. First, who's the storyteller? If he's such big game, I want to know more about him."

"Well, first of all, he's a she, an old granny called Lay Melly."

"What an odd name. Is it a title or something? Does it mean anything?"

"Melly's probably short for Emily or Amelia or something. 'Lay' could just be the old word for 'poem' . . ."

"I thought these people were peasants."

"Kath, will you please not use that word?"

"What word?"

"Peasant. This is not the Middle Ages."

"I don't see what's so wrong about it. But okay. Strike *peasant*. Next question: if the watchacallit, the gab, is so private, how come you got invited?"

"I told a hitch-hiker my girlfriend's ancestors came from around here, and I was helping you rediscover your family history."

"You shameless liar."

"Well, I had to show I wasn't a developer. So he told me about the gab. He said, 'Bring your bird.'"

"What bird? The crow?"

"It's a country word for girlfriend."

"But I'm more a stranger than you are."

"That's what I mean about the questions. Just keep mum. Don't blow my cover."

"I'll try. But it sounds more and more like a spy movie. Next question: where does Lay Melly hang out? And will there be any food? I'm starved."

"I don't know about food. Probably not, maybe tea, coffee, stuff like that. But we'll have dinner later, when we get back to the hotel. Can you last?"

"If I have to."

"As to where she hangs out, her cottage is tucked into in a cove at the cliff base just a little ways back from the sea. You go down a ravine—I hope you're not wearing heels—and cross the hump-backed bridge, and there you are."

"Say that again."

"About not wearing heels?"

"No, the about the bridge. It sounded like a poem. Or a story. Down the path across the hump-backed bridge. What is that?" She frowned, concentrating. "Bridge . . . bridge— I've got it. 'The Billy-goats Gruff.' The three

Billy-goats cross the bridge one by one, and their hooves make a noise—trip-trap, trip-trap—and the troll under the bridge says, 'Who's that trotting over my bridge? Here I come to gobble you up!'"

"Yeah," said Mick, "I remember. Each goat says don't eat me, there's a bigger one behind, and the biggest billy-goat butts the troll into the water, and he turns to stone. What's the matter now?"

Kath had gone white and was staring into invisible distance, her eyes fixed, trancelike. The change was so abrupt he didn't know what to say.

Kath was crouched under the kitchen table like the troll under the bridge, while, above her, her mother was beating cake batter in a yellow bowl. The spoon resounded — trip-trap! trip trap! — and the troll roared back in Kath's fiercest voice, "Who's that trotting over my bridge? Here I come to gobble you up!"

And then Kath screamed in terror of herself. Blind with panic, she scrambled out from under the table and fell against the legs of her mother.

17

"Kath! Honey, what's the matter?"

She buried her face in her mother's skirts "The troll." She could hardly get the word out. To say it would call it. And it would come.

Her mother murmured soothingly. "He won't get you. I won't let him."

She slipped a hand under Kath's chin, lifting her face to the twilight. "And anyway, aren't you the troll? You can't be afraid of yourself."

Kath knew better.

"Hello? What's the matter?" Mick was staring at her.

Mist eddied around the car, beaded on the windshield, drifted in the window, turned to water on her skin. She rubbed her face and looked at the damp on her fingers.

"I was . . . under a bridge."

"You scared me."

"I'm sorry. I scared myself. Have you ever done that?" *Silly question*, she thought. *Mick has never been scared of anything.*

He surprised her. "Yes, I have. When I was a kid there was this bridge, one of those old wooden ones where you can see through the cracks between the boards? I'd watch the water sliding by and sliding by underneath, and I'd feel it pulling me down. Fear of falling. That what you mean?"

"No. Fear of wanting to fall. My bridge was the one in the billy-goat story, with a troll under it."

"And you thought you were a billy-goat and it would eat you?"

"Worse than that. I was the troll."

"Aha! Little Bridget and the fairy men."

"Who are they?"

"It's a poem, 'The Fairies':

"Up the airy mountain,
Down the rushy glen,
We daren't go a-hunting
For fear of little men.

"That's the fear. But there's another verse:

"They stole little Bridget
For seven years long;
When she came down again

19

Her friends were all gone.

"That's the falling. Seven years in Elfland is a human lifetime."

"Seven years in Elfland might be worth a human lifetime. And you're a fine one to talk about Little Bridget! How about you, Mister Folklore? You spend half your time in Elfland. You don't take your own advice or you wouldn't be here right now on the trail of those stories."

"On Spiderweb Alley. But that's scholarship. That's different. Come on, Little Bridget. Time to go a-hunting."

He pulled off the road and rolled the car to rest among the trees. Headlamps shining through the mist made the little grove a midsummer night's dream seen through gauze. He switched off the lights, cut the ignition. The engine, cooling, made pinging noises against the silence.

Elfland

They got out, and Mick locked the car. The grey ribbon of the road stretched behind them. Before them, distant through the mist was another grey ribbon that Kath realized was the sea. In between, the damp earth gave off layers of scent that curled in her nostrils and dizzied her with their complexity: the musty smell of decaying logs, the rank, bitter smell of moss and green vegetation and dead leaves, the sweetness of half-hidden flowers. A tang of the sea mixed with the other smells. She looked about her. Hauntings would fit this place all right. The half-lit landscape was a demi-world balancing light and dark, reality and dream, turning shapes into their own shadows. Even solid-as-a-rock Mick looked translucent, dissolving before her eyes into the mysterious light around him. She closed her eyes against the vision, wondering if she looked as transparent to him. Probably not.

"You'd better take my arm," said Mick. "And be careful. The path is steep."

She took his arm, noticing with relief that it was real and firm and solid, part of the ordinary daylight world she thought she had lost. "This is not so bad," she told him. "If this is Elfland, I can handle it."

The way plunged into a narrow hollow flanked by rocky cliffs that rose higher and higher above their heads. The chuckle of water over stones caught Kath's ear, and she saw the glimmer of a brook threading the underbrush to the left of the path. An occasional stunted tree grew right up against the cliffs, thrusting shallow roots across the path. She reached an arm for steadiness and snatched her hand back—Ow!— some climbing plant had thorns that scratched deep. She sucked a knuckle. For a moment her fingertips had felt light, regular indentations in the rock. Mindful of the thorns, she pushed aside the tight-grown branches, exposing a portion of the rock face and feeling along it with her fingertips.

And there it was. What she saw gave her the oddest feeling in the pit of her stomach — as if she were waiting in the wings of a theatre for her cue, and someone had just pushed her and whispered, "This is where you enter." Carved into the rock at about shoulder-height was a spiral, a circular labyrinth. It was roughly a foot in diameter and shallowly pecked into the stone face. *I've seen this before*, she thought. *Where?* She stared at the spiral for several minutes before noticing that another, similar labyrinth was partly visible through the thorn tangle, this one just above the first and a little to the side. Again she pushed aside the growth. Although roughly the same size, the two carvings were not identical. The second one was shorter and fatter, and its path wound a different pattern into the heart of the maze.

She ran her fingers lightly, questioningly over the curves in the stone. "Look here, Mick," there's some kind of petroglyph or something carved in the stone."

"A petroglyph? Are you sure? How can you see with the light fading so fast? Mick tugged at her arm. Not now, Kath. It's getting too dark to see anything, and anyway we're not here to see petroglyphs. Come on."

He hurried her down the path and as she stumbled after him, all knowledge of what she had seen dropped out of her memory. Hemmed in by the cliffs, they dropped into an ever-darkening underworld. The sound of running water grew louder in Kath's ears.

"Wow, this is some rushy glen, all right. Why does Lay Melly have to live so far out of the way? Is this godforsaken path her only link to the outside world?"

"Of course it's out of the way. How else do you suppose she's managed to stay undiscovered all this time? Watch your step here." He tightened his grip on her arm. "Mind that branch."

She ducked, and felt the branch brush against her hair. They were at the bottom now, and the air carried a stronger taste of salt, the louder sound of the sea. They crossed the bridge — *trip trap! trip trap!* thought Kath — and emerged onto a shelf of rock. The rising moon had not yet topped the cliff behind them, but its glow through the mist cast an extraordinary light that transformed the scene in front of them into a black and white movie. A path led down from the shelf onto the beach whose wave-patterned shingle was broken by black rocks that hunched half out of the water.

The trolls, thought Kath. *Good thing they've turned to stone.*

The tide was ebbing, the wavelets running out with unhurried speed, leaving the shingle ripple-patterned and gleaming in the strange light. A rowboat beached in the little v-shaped cove was turned bottom-up. On the rocky shelf, a cottage, its bulging stone walls and curving thatch roof softened by the mist, melted into the landscape. A patch of rose-gold shone from a window, and the sound of voices blended with the light.

"The back door to Elfland," Kath whispered to Mick.

He steered her to the door and knocked. The voices died.

"Well then, come in," said a voice.

The door swung inward at a push. A fug of cigarette and wood smoke came to meet them, heavy with the smell of damp wool and close-packed bodies. Inside, the room was tiny, or maybe the shadows of the firelight made the space look smaller. The furnishing was minimal. A table, a few wooden chairs, a bed shoved against the back wall, a stack of fish-traps in a corner. Every available surface held people, two to a chair, jammed on the bed and perched on the table like sparrows on a branch. Faces were turned toward the door, all staring at the two of them. Remembering Mick's words, Kath was painfully aware of being a newcomer, the alien among familiars.

A man in a shabby green jacket was standing at the hearth, a steaming teapot in his hand. The jacket, patched at the elbows and worn to threads around the neck, was so shaped to his body it seemed almost a part of him. Close to the fire that was clearly the place of honor, the lady of the house sat in a rocking-chair. The bones of her skull still kept the planes of beauty under a velvet skin cross-hatched with the tracks of great age. The hands on the arms of her chair were knotted with years of use, the veins running across their backs like the deltas of rivers. Her hair, thick and springy despite her age, and wound around her head in a single braid, was the brilliant white of a sunlit cloud. Despite the warmth of the fire, a shawl was tied around her shoulders.

Mick cleared his throat. "A blessing on the house," he said, but it came out husky.

I'll bet he memorized that, thought Kath. *Mick the con artist.*

"And on the guests," said the man in the jacket. "Sit you down. There's always room." His smile was genuine, and his eyes, framed in wrinkles, looked Kath over pleasantly.

She met his gaze, and was jolted by the surge of electricity that passed between them. Her eyes widened when he gave a little nod.

Watch out, little Bridget, she told herself, *or you'll get stuck in Elfland.*

On the table, a clutch of teen-age girls took up all the space. "You lot," said the man in the jacket, "shove over and make some room." The girls made vague motions of moving, and Kath hitched up into the space provided. Mick squeezed in beside her. He flashed her a "you okay?" look, and she gave him a reassuring grin. She was beginning to enjoy herself. *This is fun*, she thought. *I haven't sat on a kitchen table in years.* She looked around the room to see if anyone had noticed. Then she decided she didn't mind if anyone had noticed. Then she realized that someone had. The man with the teapot was staring at her, not rudely, just with the natural curiosity of the totally unselfconscious, and as if he knew exactly what she was thinking. She decided that it was all right to stare back, but he held her gaze so steadily that she began to feel uncomfortable and looked away.

"Tea?" Without waiting for answer he poured steaming, tawny liquid into two mugs and passed them across.

Awkward around so many strangers, and grateful in consequence for something to do, Kath took a mug and nearly dropped it, scalded by the almost-boiling tea. The large crack down the side of the mug held possibilities of spilled tea and blisters.

A glance at the man in the green jacket told her he saw her discomfort and was amused.

She flushed, and looked away. *So much for spooking the horses. They can stare as much as they want but I'm supposed to guard my tongue and not offend anybody.* She took a cautious sip of tea, feeling the burn on her tongue and the heat all the way down. The tea was strong, with a smoky undertaste. It was warming her stomach now, banishing her tiredness and, for the moment at least, melting her irritation.

Conversation resumed. It was in English, but with a strong rural accent. She listened, simply letting the cadence and the unexpected inflections fall like music on her ears. After a bit she began to understand. Two women were trading recipes, the men talked fishing, a couple of the boys were talking about a rabbit-catching expedition, and the girls were giggling and whispering.

About the boys, probably. She looked about the room, enjoying the driftwood flames — gold and red and blue and green with sea-salt — that lighted the faces, burnishing eyes and striking a random gleam from somebody's cup held out for more tea.

She became aware that the woman in the armchair — obviously Lay Melly — still had her eyes fixed on Kath, and with an effort Kath kept her eyes steady and stared back. The woman's eyes, smoky black and lightless against the firelight, never shifted, and Kath began to feel first uncomfortable, then angry at the persistent gaze. *All right, I'm a stranger, but I don't have two heads.* Then she realized that the woman was not staring at her or at anything. She couldn't. She was blind. Feeling as if she had been caught peeking through a window, Kath looked away. Then she looked back. The woman was still staring, but her expression had changed. She understood what Kath was thinking. Almost imperceptibly, by the merest inclination of her head, she nodded. Then, without altering by a millimeter her sightless gaze, the woman reached her hand to the stick propped by her chair and poked at the fire.

It blazed up into a sudden silence as the man in the green jacket said, "Well now, hasn't anyone got a story for us? Elly, can you start us off?"

The tone of the old woman's voice surprised Kath, who had been expecting something — *well*, she thought, *something older, scrappier*. Instead, the soft lilt of Elly's voice rang like a velvet-covered bell through the room as she began to speak.

"I'll start us off," she said, "but," and here her blind eyes went from Kath to Mick and back again, "there's others here tonight with stories to tell. Here's one my old gran used to tell. Happen some of you've never heard it." She settled back in her chair and began.

The Grally Tusker

*"There was a man lived up in the woods along the cliff.
And he had three sons."*

Everybody settled back to listen, and Kath could feel the whole room focus and sharpen.

"So the oldest son said to him, 'Father, give me a hound and a hawk and a horse and I'll go seek my fortune.' So he gave him a hound and a hawk and a horse and out he went, you know, to seek his fortune. Well he rode along and rode along, and it came on to night, and he looked around for an inn, but there was none, for he was in a thick wood. So he rode along and rode along some more, and the night got darker and

darker and it began to rain, and between the rain and the dark he lost his way in the wood.

"'Well,' says he, 'this is pretty bad, but I'll not lose heart, for I have my hawk and my hound and my horse to ride on.'

"And just then he saw a light a-glimmering and shimmering between the trees.

"So up he goes, and don't you know, there's a big house, oh a great big house, big as a castle pretty near, sitting in among the trees.

"And hanging by the big front door there's a big brass horn. 'Well,' says the boy to himself, 'I'll just give that horn a blow.' So he blew a great blow on the horn, y'see, and what do you know but the door swings open. And inside is a long hallway and it went on and on just like a tunnel. And then he come out into a big room. But there's nobody there. The table laid and supper set out and a fire on the hearth. But not a soul did he see.

"So he rode right in and sat right down and ate some supper, and then he went and sat over by the fire, to dry his clothes, you know, and he had a funny **fe-e-e-**

ling, like he was being looked at, like he was being **sta-a-a-ared at**. Real hard. But he didn't see ary thing and he didn't hear ary thing. And still nobody came.

"Until it struck midnight. Then, the door opened, and in rushed t h e G r a l l y T u s k e r.

"He was **b-i-i-g**. One tusk was long and sharp like a knife and curved up at the end, and the other was broken off short and jagged and cruel, and his eyes gleamed red like a garnet stone that you find in the brook.

"Well, he sat down and he looked at the oldest son. And then he said, 'Does your horse kick a-tall?'

"'He does,' says the oldest son.

"'Here's a net to throw over him,' says the Grally Tusker. And he give him a net and the young man threw it over his horse's back.

"Then he says, 'Does your hound bite a-tall?'

"'He does,' says the young man.

"'Here's a net to throw over him,' says the Grally Tusker. And he give him a net and the young man threw it over his hound's back.

"Then he says, 'Does your hawk peck a-tall?'

"'He does,' says the young man.

"'Here's a net to throw over him,' says the Grally Tusker. And he give him a net and the young man threw it over his hawk's back. But the Grally Tusker got another net and he threw it over the young man's back and caught him fast."

She stopped. The room had been utterly still while the story unfolded, but at the last words there was a sudden, collective intake of breath, and Kath saw one of the children on the floor scoot backwards to nestle in the shelter of her mother's legs. The mother pulled the child's shoulders in and cradled them between her knees.

The silence pooled. *She certainly understands timing*, thought Kath. *I'd quit right there if it were me. But I'll bet she doesn't. We'll have* to go through the ritual three times. I know what's coming. I almost wish I didn't.

"Well, when the oldest son didn't come back, they were in a taking, you can guess. And then the second son says to his father, 'Father, give me a hound and a hawk and a horse to ride and I'll go seek my fortune.'

"So the father gave him a hound and a hawk and a horse to ride, and he went out to seek his fortune.

"Well, he rode along and rode along, and it came on to night and he looked around for an inn, but there was none, for he was in a thick wood.

"So he rode along and rode along some more, and the night got darker and darker, and it began to rain, and what with the rain and the dark he lost his way."

It rides on repetition, thought Kath. We have to repeat it to make it come out right. She looked up to meet the lightless eyes of the old woman, who was aiming the story straight at her. The blind eyes pulled her into their darkness, and the voice wrapped the darkness around her, and through it she began to hear the patter of rain on the cottage thatch. Or, was it the pattering of little feet, creatures in the magic wood? She could hear night noises outside. Or, was it her horse's hooves stirring through the wet leaves of the forest path? With the second son she rode through the dark, and began to feel the loneliness that was all around him. She was with him and she was afraid for him, innocent as he was, all unknowing of the fate that awaited him. Through his eyes she saw the light twinkling and twinkling through the dark wood. Through his eyes she saw the great house and as herself she knew what was inside it. She rode with the young man up to the door. *Don't do it*, she said inside herself, but she knew he would. He would do the things he should not do. He would take down the horn and blow a loud blast. He would go wide-eyed into the castle and sit down at the table and eat the faery food. The Grally Tusker would come in a rush and ask the questions and the second son would answer the Grally Tusker in all innocence, and he would be caught as his brother had been caught. That was the rule, the implacable force of the story.

It happened as she feared, as she felt. He sounded the horn, opened the door, ate the waiting supper, and at the appointed time the Grally Tusker, huge, with eyes that burned with red fire, came rushing into the room. The questions were asked, the answers given, the dreadful moment arrived, and the Grally Tusker threw the net over the young man and caught him in a spell.

Don't stop now, she said to the old woman, and the old woman began the third and final movement.

"When the second son didn't come back, well then, they knew something was fearfully wrong, and the youngest son said to his father, 'Father, give me a hound and a hawk and a horse and I'll go seek my fortune.' So the father — he didn't want to, but he knew he'd better — he gave him a hound and a hawk and a horse, and out he went to seek his fortune."

It really is magical, thought Kath. She looked sideways to see how Mick was taking it. He was frowning, and his lips were moving.

Trying to memorize it, she thought. She tried to imagine Mick as the oblivious third son, riding up to the house as big as a castle. She stood next to him as he blew the horn. She followed him as he went inside and down the long dark hallway. He emerged into a large room, comfortingly bright and warm and dry after the dark wood and the chill, soaking rain. Shrugging off his wet cloak, he hung it on the peg by the fireplace, where it steamed gently in the heat. On the wide hearth a fire was burning merrily but in uncanny silence, with no cheery crackle of wood or gentle rushing sound. The transparent, colorless flames looked like water. Overhead great beams lost themselves in the shadows of a soaring arched roof. In the center of the room, the long table was laid for dinner. Light from candles in the great silver candelabra picked out gleams in the silver and woke shimmers in the crystal goblets.

She saw Mick's lips move. "Here's a meal set ready," he was saying to himself, "and I've ridden long through the wood, and I'm hungry." He sat down and began to eat. Kath wondered if he knew it was faery food.

Around Mick the silence thickened, and the candle flames bent sideways like a wind had passed over them. Kath's throat tightened. She was conscious that her breath was coming fast and shallow, and she could feel the coldness in the pit of her stomach that presaged the panic she knew was about to possess her. *Here it comes*, she thought.

"In rushed the Grally Tusker, and looked at the young man. 'Does your horse kick a-tall?' he asked.

"'He does,' said the third son.

"'Here's a net to throw over him,' says the Grally Tusker. And he give him a net and the young man threw it on the fire and the fire hissed and sent up a great cloud of smoke.

"'What's that hissing?' says the Grally Tusker.

"'It's just the sap bubbling in the pine logs,' says the third son.

"'Does your hound bite a-tall?' he asked.

"'He does,' said the third son.

"'Here's a net to throw over him,' says the Grally Tusker. And he give him a net and the young man made to throw it on the fire but secretly he hid it behind him. And there was a great cracking and crying.

"'What's that cracking and crying?' says the Grally Tusker.

"'It's just the knots popping in the pine logs,' says the third son.

"'Does your hawk peck a-tall?' asked the Grally Tusker.

"'He does,' said the third son.

"'Here's a net to throw over him,' says the Grally Tusker. And he give him a net and the young man made to throw it on the fire, but secretly hid it behind him. And the fire roared up the chimney like **thu-n-n-nder**.

"'What's that roaring and thundering?' says the Grally Tusker.

"'It's just the wood blazing up in the pine logs,' says the third son.

"And at that the Grally Tusker rushed upon the third son!

"But the third son took the nets and flung them over the Grally Tusker, so he couldn't move. Then he called to his horse and his hound and his hawk, and his horse kicked out and his hound bit down and his hawk pecked out the eyes, and all together they killed the Grally Tusker.

"Then the third son went looking through the castle and found the enchanter's wand. It was disguised as a flowering branch heavy with apple-blossoms, but it was a wand sure enough and the third son waved it to free the older sons from the wicked enchantment of the net. They packed up all his gold and treasure and took it home to their father and they lived happy and died happy and may all of us here tonight do the same.

"The tide has run. My story's done."

Taking Leave

Kath felt a touch on her shoulder, and turned to see a strange face regarding her anxiously. It was the third son.

"You all right? Kath?"

She stared at him blankly. "Am I . . . what?"

It was Mick, and he was asking her a question, but his words were meaningless. She was out of time and space and didn't know where or who she was. She was losing it, feeling it fade with the swiftness of dream. It was dissipating like mist, and she couldn't hold it.

"He's dead, isn't he?"

"What? What do you mean, dead? Who's dead? Where?"

"The Grally Tusker. In the castle. You killed him . . ." She blinked, hesitated. "I mean, . . . what did you say?"

"I said, 'are you all right?' You're dead white, and your eyes . . ."

She stared blankly at him, shook her head to clear cobwebs. And then she came back to Kath sitting on a table in a shabby cottage. "Oh for heaven's sake, Mick," she said impatiently. "Of course I'm all right. Why ever wouldn't I be?"

There was the shuffling sound of children squirming, people getting up to stretch. The woman with the baby stood up. The child was sound asleep, and she found a place for it among the cuddled bodies on the bed in the corner. The man in the green jacket was looking at Kath. She turned away from him toward Mick, and said again, "Why wouldn't I be?"

"I don't know," said Mick. "I just thought . . . you just looked funny."

Now why was she so angry?

"You were so still I thought you were falling asleep, but your eyes were wide open and staring. I thought you were going to pass out."

"I'm perfectly all right. Really."

"If you say so. Look, do you want to leave?"

"No, of course not. Do you?"

"No. But you're the one who said she was hungry."

"I'm not hungry anymore. I want to stay."

More tea was brewed, poured, drunk, more stories told. There was one about a girl who danced all night at the fair with a boy from another village, and the next morning she found out he'd been killed in a fight the day before. Someone told about the castle at the bottom of the sea where there is a banquet every day. Another told about the girl who got adopted by the pig-goddess. There was one about an inn that haunted itself, burning down and coming back and burning down and coming back. There was one about a story-teller who never finished any story but the last one about a story-teller who never finished any story. Mick listened with cataloging concentration. Kath rode the stories like a wave. It was past midnight when the evening ended.

When she stood up to go, Kath found her feet had gone to sleep, and she nearly fell over.

Mick was already saying his goodnight, thanking his hostess. He was careful to address her formally by name, conferring it as a title. The blind gaze looked at him for a long minute, and then her head turned the least bit toward Kath standing beside him.

"You'll forgive an old woman not getting up? My legs are that lame. But I've had pleasure in your visit, my dear. You'll come again." It was not a question.

How does she do that? Kath wondered. *She doesn't see me; how did she know where I was?* "Thank you. I would like to come again. Goodbye . . . " She was hesitant to use the odd-sounding title; it didn't seem right.

"Call me Elly, my dear, that's what everyone around here does."

"Goodbye, then, Elly."

The man in the green jacket held out both hands. "Come on then, Elly," he said.

She stretched her hands, and he heaved her out of the chair, which rocked a little, gently, at her departure. He supported her across the room, all the while calling over his shoulder, "Good night, then. Good night. Come again."

They were out in the cool night lit by a setting moon. They crossed the little humpbacked bridge, but Kath was still in Elfland.

"What an evening. Thank you, Mick. I wouldn't have missed it for anything. Uh, that guy . . . in the green jacket? The one sitting next to Elly. Was that your hitch-hiker?"

"Yeah, that was him. Why?"

Kath thought of that electrical moment. "No special reason. I just wondered."

They started up the narrow gully, the sound of water on the right hand now. The moon was low, and as they ascended it seemed to tangle in the tree branches behind them — a glimmering and shimmering — like the lights of a distant castle. Kath felt her imagination sliding. *Stop it, Kath, don't let the dark run away with you. It's just a story.*

Mick was puffing up the slope of the path. "You seem to have made a hit. I didn't notice her giving me any invitation to come back. May I come with you next time?"

"Don't get your nose out of joint. She was just being nice. And besides . . . " She laughed.

"What's so funny?"

"You're so funny. 'Lay Melly' for heaven's sake! I thought when you told me it sounded like a crazy kind of name. Her name's Lame Elly. Didn't you hear her say she was lame, hear her tell me to call her Elly?"

He had the grace to laugh. "Elly, Melly, whatever. I guess I'm not used to the accent or the dialect or whatever. Clever of you to notice that."

He changed the subject. "Well, what did you think?"

"Of the stories?"

"No, of her."

"I thought she was the most extraordinary ordinary person I've ever seen. She seems like just an old woman in a shawl, and then she gets into a story, and wow! Do you think it has to do with her being blind?"

"Is she blind? I didn't notice."

"How could you not notice? Well, maybe she didn't stare at you."

"Now, wait a minute. I thought you said she was blind."

"She is."

"Then how could she stare at me or you or anybody?"

"I don't know, but she did. She stared right at me. That's how I saw she was blind. Maybe that has something to do with how she tells a story. She sees with her mind's eye."

"I don't see how being blind would make any difference."

"I liked the first story best, the one about the whaddyacallit, the Tusky."

"Tusker. Grally Tusker. It's the standard pattern—three trials, third son, some sort of monster. But you're right. It's the way she tells it as much as the story itself. The style, the pauses, the spin she puts on things." He went on talking. "Actually, that's the problem for a collector. The thing you can't get on paper. And the body language — not that she had much of that. Still as a statue all the time she was talking. Of course, if she's blind . . . And style is tricky to reproduce, especially style like hers, those quirky pauses and up-and-down intonations. But I can get the language, the words."

"What does 'Grally' mean?"

"No clue. Probably something like 'great' or 'chief.' Not just any old tusker, but the *Grally* Tusker. The head honcho. What did it mean to you?"

"Something growly and gravelly. A lot of it was her voice, the way she said 'Grraallyy.' What kind of monster do you suppose a Grally Tusker is?"

"Something with teeth, that's for sure. Tusks, after all. A very big baddie. Whatever's hiding under the bed, or in the dark closet, or in the woods."

The woods. Kath closed her eyes, but had to open them again to keep from stumbling.

"It's all theory to you, isn't it? I bet you've never met a Grally Tusker in your life."

"I've met a lot of them. Just about every book . . . "

"Oh, books! I mean really met one. You spend so much time chasing stories, you never look under the bed or in the closet."

"What's wrong with chasing stories? They get lost if somebody doesn't. Besides, there are Grally Tuskers running about loose. They don't all live under the bed or in the closet. Or in castles."

"Okay then, Mr. Folklore, what or who is THE Grally Tusker?"

He grinned. "A big bad billy-goat eater. With knobs on. A giant animal, a boar or a wolf or a big dog. Teeth. What did you see?"

She closed her eyes, recollecting. "I'm not sure I saw. It was — he was — too big for seeing. When he came rushing in I just got a feeling."

"What sort of feeling?"

"Power, mostly. Raw. A big bad billy-goat eater — with knobs on. I hope this one stays under his bridge," she murmured, "I sure don't want to meet him."

"Tired of Elfland already, are you, Bridget?"

"I surrender. I've had all the haunting I can stand for one night."

They were nearly at the top now. She looked again at the moon glimmering through the trees like a beckoning light in a window, but Mick went on unheeding.

"That Elly knows how to weave a spell. A net to throw over us. How many times do you suppose she's told that story?"

"Does it matter? It wasn't a performance. She was telling from the heart. Could you do that? Not just hear it and write it down, but feel it?"

"Not at the moment, Little Bridget. I've had enough story-telling."

The path leveled out as they neared the top, and the darkness became marginally lighter as they neared the road. Mick rummaged in his pocket for his car key.

Out of this Wood
Do Not Desire to Go

"Mick, where's the car?"

"Just up ahead. I remember I noticed a little circle of trees to the left."

"I don't see any circle, and I don't see any car."

"You're not looking. I said left, not right."

"I'm looking left. And I don't see any car."

"Well it's right over . . . That's funny. I could have sworn I remembered the place. I know I marked it. Guess I've forgotten all my camping lore. We must have swung too far to one side when we got to the top of the path. It's so dark, and the path is so faint I keep losing track. There aren't that many places to park in these woods. I think it's just up this way."

He led off walking briskly, and she followed. In less than a minute he slowed down, then stopped, brushing a hand across his face. "Spiderweb Alley."

"What? What did you say?"

"Nothing. I just walked into a spiderweb. But I thought the road was closer. We weren't very far in when I parked. I was going to get my bearings from the road and then backtrack."

"I think it's the other way."

"Why?"

"I don't know. A feeling. This way doesn't feel right."

"Okay, I'm willing to go back, but are you sure of where you're going? We don't want to just blunder around the woods. We'd get lost in no time."

"The moon was in the west when we left the cottage. I remember seeing the light on the water. And we came more or less straight up the hill. If we go back toward where the moon was, but a little over that way, we ought to come pretty close."

Slowly and carefully they retraced their steps, checking direction against a moon already sinking low behind the tree trunks. As they moved, its dimming light more than ever looked like a flickering candle set in a distant window in the wood. Kath kept a tight hold on her imagination.

Mick slowed again. "Kath, stop. We've gone too far now. I'm sure we're past the circle of trees. Dammit, this isn't some monster parking garage in the city, it's a strip of wood in the middle of nowhere! How could we lose the car?"

It was a question he asked himself again and again with mounting irritation as they blundered and circled and doubled back through a wood that seemed determined to confuse them. The moon set, robbing them not only of light but any sure way of reckoning direction. Treetops laced themselves without pattern, and the star-scattered sky gave them no guidance. The ground was no better. Siren shapes that promised to be the car turned out to be overgrown tangles of underbrush that scratched them and snagged their sleeves. Trees came and planted themselves directly in the middle of whatever faint track they followed, and tendrils of nameless vines caught at their sleeves.

At least it's not raining, thought Kath. *Thank God for good weather. We don't have to do this ~~and~~ get soaked, that's one thing*. Talking briskly inside her head, she controlled her growing uneasiness as best she could, tamping down flickers of panic at unidentified noises, refusing to catch her breath at sudden distant rustlings and furtive movements among the leaves. The climax came when they found themselves once again in the same little clearing marked by the same recognizably misshapen tree they had passed on several previous circuits.

Mick exploded, unleashing a series of curses that increased exponentially in tone and volume. Finally, he kicked the tree. "WHERE IN HELL IS THE BLOODY CAR?"

She waited for the air to stop vibrating. "It's wherever we left it. It didn't just drive off by itself. Look, Mick, we're not getting anywhere, we're just making ourselves dizzy stumbling around in circles. Why don't we quit for now? I feel like I'm getting to know this tree. Let's just stay here and wait till daylight when we'll have a better chance of finding the car."

"But it's got to be here. If we keep looking we're bound to find it."

"Mick, I'm going cross-eyed peering into the dark. Right now I wouldn't see the car if I fell over it. But if you don't want to stay here, how about going back down to the cottage?"

"You mean wake them up to tell them we've lost the car? No thanks."

"Just a suggestion. I don't like the idea of waking people up at this time of night any more than you do. So let's just stay right here."

"Are you proposing that we spend the night in a clearing in the middle of the woods?"

"Yes. I am proposing that we spend the night — what's left of it anyway — in a clearing in the woods. Why not? At least we know this clearing. We've gone through it at least three times. Besides, what else is there to do? There probably isn't that much of the night left anyway. I can't see my watch, but I'd guess it's somewhere around two a. m. It's midsummer, thank goodness, so it'll start getting light in a couple of hours. It's not cold, not very cold anyway. I don't suppose we'll sleep, but we can at least sit down and catch our breath."

He rubbed a hand across his face. "Sorry, Kath. I know I haven't been behaving very well.

I'm mad and tired and frustrated, and this is not the way I planned for the evening to end. You're probably as tired as I am, besides which it's way past dinner time and I promised you."

"I'm way past hungry. But I am tired. Make that exhausted. That's why I want to stop for now."

"Well in that case we might as well stay right where we are. It's as good as anyplace else. And no bears or boars. Or Grally Tuskers."

I wish you hadn't said that, she thought. *Now I'll dream about the Grally Tusker, I know I will. If I get any sleep at all. Which I doubt.*

"If we're going to stay here, let's do it right. Lie down. Here, put this under your head." He took off his sweater and rolled it into a pillow. "No extra covers. Good thing it's a warm night."

She wriggled herself a nest in the fallen leaves and propped her head on the sweater.

"What will you put under your head?"

"Oh, I'll find a rock or something. Us nature boys are tough." He eased himself down at the foot of the tree.

Quiet settled around them.

"Mick?"

"What?"

"I still think it was a wonderful evening. I wouldn't have missed it for anything."

"Good," he said. "Me either. Do you think you can sleep?"

"I can try. How about you?"

"I'll keep watch. Us nature boys don't sleep."

"Okay."

"Okay."

Mick fell at once into sleep, and Kath could hear his breathing, light at first and then settling into a regular puffing, a reassuringly human sound. She was vaguely aware that the wood had fallen silent. Now she could hear the little night noises starting again. Insects chirped and clicked and buzzed. A sleepy bird called and then was silent. A small animal on a night hunt rustled furtively through the underbrush. Tired as she was, she lay wide-eyed, looking up through the blackness of the leaves. *I knew I wouldn't sleep,* she thought. A rock was lodged under her left shoulder blade. She fished it out and tossed it aside. It landed in the fallen leaves with a soft thunk. The little noise instantly put a stop to all the other noises. The wood fell silent again. She wondered if she had disturbed some animal that wouldn't take kindly to being wakened, but nothing stirred, so she lay back and tried to get comfortable and stared at the leaves again. The silence thickened.

Then she heard a sound, faraway and faint, but very clear. Something big was moving about in the distant underbrush. She lay very still and listened. Gradually, very gradually, the sound grew in force and intensity. Then it was definitely coming nearer. It seemed to get larger as well as louder, and she had a sense of something huge rampaging down the forest aisles, rushing toward her. She came up on one elbow, wide-eyed and staring into the darkness, feeling her heart thump so heavily it shook her ribcage.

I ought to wake Mick, she thought, but she simply stayed frozen and waited, hypnotized, paralyzed, for whatever it was. The sound, unnaturally clear and sharp in the still night, neared and loudened and then, just as whatever it was seemed about to come bursting into the little clearing, the crashing lessened and receded, and she realized that whatever it was had passed to one side and was now moving away from her. Perhaps she was not the quarry after all. The crashing sound diminished and died to nothing. A tide of silence flowed back.

After a minute she lay down again and waited for her heart to go back to its normal pace. *I am not afraid*, she thought. *I will not panic. I will not wake Mick. I am a grown woman, and this is not a fairy tale, and there is nothing to be afraid of. After all, it was my idea, staying in these woods. We could have gone back down to the cottage and waked somebody up. We could have borrowed a lantern or something. We could have asked somebody to help us look.*

Then she heard it again, returning from wherever it had gone. This time the sound was unbelievably loud and immediate and overpowering. *How could anything make so much noise?* She pictured a tank, a steamroller, a trailer truck, anything ludicrous and out of place that would help her to laugh and see how ridiculous the whole thing must be. None of it worked; the crashing sound was too real, too present, too . . . *yes, primitive!* . . . to be part of the modern world. It created its own time, and she was in it, waiting in a wood unimaginably old for the arrival of — *of what?* — the ancient beast, the raw savagery. The Grally Tusker. In a minute she would see it break through the thicket and rush, huge and red-eyed, into the

61

little clearing. And throw a net over her. She couldn't breathe.

Abruptly the noise ceased. But the silence was, if anything, more pervasive. Certainly it was more ominous, more unbearable. She knew she was being watched. Whatever it was that was out there, hiding in the darkness just outside her range of vision, it was staring intently at her. The gaze went on and on. Something was about to happen. Someone or some thing was about to burst out of the trees. In a minute she would break, call out, scream. But she was struck dumb, mute. She couldn't scream until she saw what it was.

Opening Time

"Kath, I hate to wake you."

Mick's voice came down a long tunnel from another country. She opened her eyes, blinked, saw him bending over her.

"I know it's early, but the day's here already, and we'd better get started."

He pulled her to her feet. More mist had come in, covering the world with translucent white, and damping their hair and clothes. Drops of moisture pearled on leaves and turned spiderwebs into fairy necklaces strung with pearls. They walked a few yards to the car sitting where they had left it, in the circle of trees less than a stone's throw from the road.

"Well, I'll be damned," said Mick. "We must have walked past it a dozen times last night and never saw it. I've done that with books I was looking for on the shelf, but never anything as big as a car. Makes me feel stupid."

Not stupid, thought Kath. *Haunted.*

They drove silently. The air smelled of salt and seaweed and wet stone. The mist was thick, and Mick slowed the car to make sure he stayed with the road. The trees on either side showed like dim sentinels as the mists wandered in the sea wind. Sometimes Kath could see trunks standing still and silent. And then in an eyeblink the mist would condense into a wall encircling the car, shutting them in a little room. Mick switched on the headlights. Kath kept looking for breaks in the wall. Then she saw something move, an indeterminate shape shifting behind and through the mist. It was pacing the car.

"Mick, do you see that?"

"See what?"

"A shape. I don't know. Like a . . . a hollow in the mist. A shadow behind the trees."

"I don't see anything."

"There. On my side of the road. Like a big animal. A Baskerville hound. Or a Grally Tusker. Now it's gone."

"I wouldn't worry about it. The mist plays tricks with your eyes."

I'm not worried, Kath told herself. *But it wasn't mist playing tricks. I saw something.* The shadowy shape stayed in her mind, and she imagined she could hear the muffled sound of something bulky moving in the underbrush, keeping pace with the car, tracking it. With an effort, she changed her focus. *Do I look as rumpled and dirty as I feel? Worse, probably. I'd like to wash my face and hands. And brush my teeth. And get into clean clothes.* She thought of her suitcase back at the hotel. Glancing at Mick, she saw the beginnings of stubble on his chin, leaves and twigs in his hair, and the hair itself, usually neatly combed, sticking out in bristles. *A couple of tramps*, she thought. *People will do more than stare when they see us. They'll run the other way.*

One hand on the wheel, Mick fished in his back pocket, and handed her his comb.

"Your hair's a mess."

She managed a smile. "Don't you know that's one of the things you should never tell a woman? Besides, you're no beauty yourself."

She reached up and pulled a twig out of his hair. "Here," she said, handing him the twig. "Badge of survival."

With a magician's flourish he plucked something out of her hair and held it out, a crumpled flower, small and white, with pointed petals.

"We both survived," he said. "And we've got the badges to prove it."

She cradled the flower in her hand for a moment, then carefully stuck it back in her hair, where Mick thought it looked like the first star in an evening sky. He started to tell Kath and then had to negotiate a sharp turn, and when the road was running straight again he had forgotten all about it.

The sea wind was blowing the mist into rags now, and through the rags there appeared the ghost of a building. Set back from the road, it wavered in and out of sight as the wayward mist alternately thickened and thinned, erasing and redrawing the outlines. Now you see it now you don't. It didn't look real, much less open, but Mick turned into the gravel car park anyway. A signboard swinging from a post by the gate announced "The Wicken Tree — Inn and Public House." A matching sign, of the tree with an outline of the house behind it, swung above the front doorway. The house itself had irregular fieldstone walls, a tall stone chimney at one end, windows and gables set at uneven heights. In the yard an old-fashioned well with a peaked canopy and a bucket on a chain sat next to a large flat stump.

Kath looked at the stump. "I'll bet you anything that used to be the Wicken Tree," she said. "The whole place looks like an illustration in a fairy tale book. There should be a Mother Goose in the doorway dressed in an apron and mobcap and leaning on a stick."

"All ready for tourists," said Mick. He got out and went over to the well. Peering down, he saw only emptiness. "Dry as a bone," he announced. "Just for show." He mounted the stone steps, hollowed by time and the wearing of long-gone feet, and peered through the pane in the front door. The hallway was unlighted, but he rapped anyway, and a woman in a green apron appeared at the door. The look on her face was impatient.

"We're closed, can't you see? We don't open till ten." She was about to shut the door in his face when, looking over his shoulder, her eyes widened, and her face changed from irritation to concern.

"Oh. Well now. That's different."

Wondering what was different, Mick turned to see Kath slumped against the side of the car. Her face was paper-white, and she was blinking dizzily.

"Better bring her inside," said the woman. "Feeling ill, is she?"

"Well, yes, a bit. Not exactly ill, more just tired, I think."

He went to Kath and put his hands on her shoulders. "You all right? You look awfully pale."

The woman was watching them intently, all annoyance erased. "She needs to sit down. She's ready to fall."

They stepped inside, into the cool dark of the hallway, and she closed the door behind them. A large wooden clock hanging on the wall just inside the door chimed the hour and then struck ten.

"You said you were closed," said Mick, "but your clock just said you were open."

She shrugged. "It does that," she said. "Thinks it's always opening time. Pay no attention."

She steered them into the common room and settled them at a booth. The paneled room was cool and dim, smelling of beer and smoke and late evenings. Kath collapsed into the booth's corner, tilted her head back and closed her eyes.

"Looks peaky doesn't she?" said the woman. "I'll get some tea." She disappeared.

Kath spoke with eyes still shut. "Sorry, Mick. I just felt dizzy for a minute. I'll be all right."

"I'm not so sure of that. You seem pretty shaky to me. No food and not much sleep. When did you eat last?"

She opened her eyes. "Been so long I have to stop and think. Breakfast yesterday, I guess, but that was just coffee. I didn't have time for lunch what with packing and getting to the station and everything. And then the journey."

"And then you got here and you missed dinner because I hustled you to get to the gab, and from there we crashed around in the woods for God knows how long. Which adds up to no lunch, and no dinner. A clean sweep. I'm sorry, Kath. I've been a pig. I don't care if it's too early. I'm going to talk Mother Goose into giving us breakfast."

"Here you are." The woman was back with two steaming cups. "Tea is what you need, love. Drink this and you'll feel a bit better. You make sure she drinks it all." This to Mick.

He seized the opportunity. "What she really needs is some food. She's had nothing to eat since yesterday morning. Do you think you could . . .?"

He never got a chance to finish. "Nothing to it. She's most welcome. And you too, of course. Eggs and ham all right? And toast to go with. Jam as well, I expect. Or honey. I'll be back. Don't you go anywhere."

Mick thanked her, and she vanished through a green door into what must be the kitchen. He turned back to Kath, who was drinking the tea thirstily. A faint color was coming back to her cheeks.

"How about another cup?"

"Do you think you could talk her into some coffee? Tea's all right, but . . . "

"Coming up."

He pushed his way through the green door into the kitchen, a large room whose stone-flagged floor was brightened by a scatter of braided rungs. Above his head wooden beams hung with strings of garlic and drying herbs spanned the room. An open fireplace occupied one end of the room, its opposite dominated by a painted dresser stacked with plates and bowls and platters sufficient to serve an army. The two adjoining walls held on one side a deep clay sink and on the other a vast range whose many burners looked sufficient to cook for a host of hungry feeders. Their hostess was standing at the big wooden table in the center of the room and cracking eggs into a bowl with the double-handed expertise of long practice. She was ordinary-enough looking, a bit on the bony side but not gaunt, with rusty hair greying at the temples and straggling out of a bun at the back. Rusty voice to match the hair. About fifty or so, he guessed. Only the eyes were distinctive, soft black and lightless in a depth that saw everything but gave away nothing, set in a lined and ruddy face that otherwise resembled a hundred other country faces.

The ghosts of cooking odors hung in the air: roasting meats and rich sauces, baking breads and the spicy sweetness of pies and cakes. In more immediate range, slices of ham were curling and crisping in a skillet on the stove. The smell of these, and the aroma rising from the large tin coffeepot reminded Mick that he too hadn't eaten in a long time.

"Um, ah, Mrs. . . ?"

"Call me Greenie, dear. Everyone does."

"Greenie it is. My name's Mick."

"Short for Michael, is it?"

"Mick'll do. Look, Greenie, could you . . . I mean, is there any chance of coffee to go with the eggs and ham? Seeing as it's breakfast?"

"I'm brewing a fresh pot right now. The tea was just to get her started. I'll bring the coffee in with the eggs, pot and all. Unless you'd like a cup first?"

Without waiting for answer she reached a large cup from the dresser, poured coffee strong and fragrant, splashed a dollop of milk, added two spoons of sugar, stirred briskly and handed him the result.

It was all done before he had time to say "no thank you." He took his coffee black no sugar, but to refuse would have been churlish, considering that the place wasn't open yet, and she was making breakfast just for them. "Thanks, Greenie. Can I have one for Kath? She takes it black, no sugar."

"Kath, is it? Kath and Mick. Here you are, then. Though if you ask me that's not the best thing to put in an empty stomach."

He left her talking, smiled over his shoulder, and carried two cups of coffee back to where Kath slumped, eyes closed.

"Wakey, wakey. Here's coffee, and breakfast is coming. If you can stay awake long enough to eat, I'll get us back to the hotel, and we can both sack out. I'm pretty dead too."

With an effort she opened her eyes. "I was thinking, do you suppose they'd have a room here? I don't think I can face another drive over that road."

"What, with no luggage? No toothbrush or face creams or whatnot?"

"Just for today. Please, Mick?"

Something in her voice . . . he looked carefully at her. Something was seriously amiss, something beyond the disarray and fatigue of their night in the woods. She wasn't as well as she insisted—that was obvious—but Greenie had seen it where he hadn't, and he kicked himself for having been too willing to accept Kath's own assessment of her health. Her unwonted thinness made the planes of her face stand out too sharply under a skin normally smooth as cream but now taut with exhaustion. There was a line across her forehead. *Worry? Anxiety?* It was more than just hunger and lack of a good night's sleep.

"Sure, if you like. If they have a room, we'll take it. I'll get you tucked up in bed and then go pick up our stuff and bring it back here. You look washed out."

"I'll be better with some food. Ah." She looked up as Greenie materialized with a laden tray.

"Here you are. And here's the coffee, all hot, so just help yourselves."

She slid dishes onto the table: a platter of softly scrambled eggs, another with slices of ham crisped and curling at the edges, a plate of fried tomatoes, a rack of toast, a dish of butter, a fat little pot with raspberry jam and another with dark gold honey, a thermos jug of coffee.

"Now mind you make her eat. I'd start with toast if I was you."

The food was good. Following orders, Kath started with a piece of toast liberally buttered and spread with honey. That and even more of the coffee went a long way toward reviving her.

Mick attacked the eggs, moved on to the ham, topped those off with the tomatoes, and washed the lot down with coffee. It was steaming and strong, and he had three cups. Halfway through the tomatoes he looked at Kath's plate.

"You're not eating."

"I am."

"So what's that still on your plate?"

"I'm about to start on my second piece of toast. Just taking a break."

She looked at Mick over the rim of her cup. "I do feel better. I guess I was pretty empty. She was right — whatsername."

"Greenie. When she comes back we'll ask about a room. You really ought to finish that toast. And have some eggs."

"I will in a minute. Mick, last night . . ."

"I'm really sorry Kath . . ."

"No, no, I'm not complaining. I loved the stories, and I wanted to stay. But afterward . . . I just wondered . . . I wanted to ask . . . did you sleep all right?"

"Surprisingly enough, yes. I dropped right off. Woke up with the mist shining like cotton through the trees. How about you? You were out like a light when I roused you."

"That's just it. I wasn't out, or if I was it was just barely. Mick . . ." she hesitated, then went on, "the oddest thing happened. I heard something, like a big animal crashing around in the woods. It came right up to where we were, and it was looking at us. I could feel it. I just wondered . . . did you hear anything?"

"No, nothing. And I don't think you did either. My guess is you were dreaming."

"I wasn't asleep."

"Sure looked like it to me. All the stuff we heard at the gab swirling around in your head, it's no wonder you dreamed you were hearing things."

"My eyes were wide open. And my ears. I distinctly heard something. It went rushing past, and it was quiet for a while. And then it turned around and came back." She was gripping her cup so tightly that the coffee sloshed. He took the cup from her hand and set it down.

"To start with, there aren't any big animals around here. There haven't been deer for ages: they're all inland and up in the hills."

"How about, um, cows, or wild pigs? Boars?"

"Kath, you are the end. I wish I had your imagination. First you see a dog that isn't there, now it's a wild boar. A Grally Tusker? Permit me to doubt. And anyway, no large animal would stay that close to a road. You were dreaming. I've had dreams like that myself, where I dream I'm awake. They can seem very real. But they're just dreams."

She looked at him looking at her, and felt her usual frustration. He was being rational, as always. So clear-eyed, so logical, so unshakably the voice of reason. There was no point in arguing. She tried a different tack.

"Maybe I was dreaming, daydreaming what the story would be like if I was in it. Or not even me, but just what if the sons had been daughters instead? Would the story turn out differently? Those stories are always about young men and their adventures. If the Grally Tusker had rushed in and seen a woman — what might have happened?"

"That's an interesting question."

Now that the discussion was on a theoretical footing he was more than willing to give it some thought.

"Well, it would be mixing up the functions, and that doesn't happen. There are rules, you know. Fairy tales follow a pattern. Why?"

She shrugged. "I just wondered. Women in fairy tales are so dumb. They do stupid things—prick their finger, or eat a poisoned apple, or lose a slipper. They may sleep for a hundred years, or die after one bite, but they don't take control."

"Oh come now. Of course they do. You're talking about just the famous ones that everybody knows. Look at 'Bluebeard,' or 'Donkeyskin.' Or 'The Frog Prince.' The girls in those stories did things."

"Yes, of course, or there wouldn't have been any story. But they're always reactive. They either trick the villain, like the wife in 'Bluebeard,' or run away, like the girl in 'Donkeyskin,' or mistreat a frog like that spoiled princess. Can't they act on their own?"

"You want to meet the Grally Tusker on your own? You're braver than I am."

"Not brave, just curious. If I wrote a fairy story I'd try for something unexpected, a whole different kind of confrontation.'

"Then it wouldn't be a fairy story. These things follow patterns, you know. They don't come out of nowhere."

"Just you wait, Mr. Know-it-all. Some day I may surprise you."

"Anything more?" Greenie was back. "Top up the coffee? Or shall I clear?" She cocked her head on one side and looked critically at Kath.

"Well, you look a way sight better than you did, even though you didn't finish your eggs. Sure you don't want them?"

Kath shook her head.

"Some color in your cheeks, anyway. Food's the best medicine, I always say. Still a bit wobbly, though, aren't you dear?"

"A lot better, thank you. The food was wonderful. Um, Mick and I were talking . . . do you have rooms, that is . . . "

"On vacation are you?"

"Yes."

"No."

"Well, sort of." They both spoke at once.

Kath won. "I'm on vacation. Mick's here to do some work. He's a folk . . . "

Hastily, Mick intervened. "I'm interested in out-of-the way places. Real getaways. We went to a gab last night. Great fun."

Greenie nodded. "Aye, they're grand evenings. That would have been down at Sea

79

Cottage. I wanted to go, but someone had to mind the place."

"About that room . . . "

"We only have six — three on the first floor, two single and one double, and three just like those on the second — but I'm afraid they're all taken right now. People here for the Solstice."

"Just for tonight?" Mick coaxed, "So Kath can catch up on her sleep."

Greenie looked at Kath. "She needs to catch up on more than sleep." She looked at Mick. "Right, then. I do have one extra space, but so small it's really not even there. Hardly space to turn around, and tucked right up under the rooftree. But it has a bed to lie down, and she'd get some rest, which is what she needs. Will I show you, then?"

"Wherever it is, we'll take it," said Mick.

Greenie led them up a staircase to a long hall with doors on either side, then up a second flight to another hall. At the far end of this hall was a low, narrow door that Kath took for a linen cupboard. It was this door, however, that Greenie led them to. She produced a key from her apron pocket and, with some difficulty — for the lock was stiff and rusted — she unlocked the door and pulled it open. The space thus revealed was no cupboard but a spiral stair closed off by another narrow door. Greenie unlatched it and pushed it open. Ducking their heads under the doorframe, they walked straight into a spiderweb strung from side to side across the entrance. When the strands were disentangled, they saw a room hardly bigger than a linen cupboard. It smelled of dust and shadows and the faint fragrance of old wood. A narrow bed, a small washstand with mirror, and a wooden chair were all the furnishings, and the wide boards of the floor, as worn and cracked as those of the stairs, were innocent of rug or runner. A deeply recessed dormer window opened one wall.

"I told you it was small," said Greenie. "When they rebuilt the inn after the fire — that was long before my time, of course, ages ago — they tucked this up under the rooftree. We don't usually let it, as I said."

"It'll do just fine," Mick told her. "Won't it, Kath?"

He glanced at her. "Kath?" Louder, "Kath! Hey Kath! You all right?"

He put his hand on her arm. She turned, coming up out of deep water, looked at him blankly for a moment, then gave a shaky laugh.

"I'm fine, Mick. I just thought I heard something . . . faraway, like a big animal crashing around in the underbrush." She shrugged. "Probably nothing."

"Sure you're okay, Kath?"

She nodded, then gave a little shiver and hugged her arms around her elbows. She felt a chill settle in her bones, air from another time, as if the room had been shut away from the rest of the house for centuries, waiting.

"Brrr. It's dead cold in here. I should have worn your sweater, Mick."

"Doesn't feel chilly to me," Mick said. "Matter of fact it's bit stuffy, tucked up under the roof like this. Mind if I open the window?" He glanced at Greenie, who was looking at Kath and did not answer.

"I said do you mind . . ."

"What?"

"Is it all right if I open the window?"

"Better let me do it. It may stick. It hasn't been opened in a while, and it's a bit stiff." Greenie unlatched the shutters and lifted the sash.

Kath got a view over the carpark, and a glimpse of trees that she guessed would lead to the sea.

"It still feels cold," said Kath.

"I'll fetch some blankets," said Greenie quickly. "You'll be needing them for tonight anyway. Won't take a minute."

She disappeared, chattering, and returned with two woolen blankets. One she folded on the chair, the other she laid across the foot of the bed. "Just pull that around you and you'll warm right up." Her voice floated back to them as she disappeared down the stairs. "The bathroom's down one flight, at the end of the hall."

Mick gave Kath a gentle push "Okay, lady. Into bed."

Kath toed off her shoes, shucked her shirt and jeans, draped them over the chair, flung back the coverlet and slid into the bed. It felt good to stretch out with a mattress under her instead of roots and rocks and branches. She snuggled down, nestled her head on the pillow, and waved a yawning goodbye to Mick.

He shook out the blanket and laid it over her like a benison. "I'll back in a few hours," he told her. "You sleep as long as you like and tonight I'll make good on that dinner."

Kath nodded, hearing the door click shut softly. She snuggled down under the blanket and, as she sank fathoms deep into dark, dreamless sleep, the room disappeared, and the clock downstairs struck ten.

A Room with a View

Kath's eyes opened. She was abruptly, totally awake, clear-eyed and alert. She sat up. How long had she been asleep? Her watch confirmed her worst suspicion: she hadn't been out more than ten minutes. The air was so crystalline that she had the sensation of looking at another world than the one she lived in, a world made of cut glass whose edges were clearer and sharper than the ones she knew. The contrast both disturbed and excited her, and she felt an urge to escape from her old world to the one that awaited her. The little attic room was a portal, the passageway between the worlds. She felt the room watching her. *No, not the room. Somebody.* Out of the corner of her eye she saw an arm reach toward her, and felt a jolt of terror, only to have the arm turn into a shadow on the wall that was a tree branch blowing in the wind. She tried to laugh but her knees had gone weak. She made herself look at the shadow again. *No one there. Silly.* She reached for jeans and shirt, and glancing in the mirror, ran her fingers through her hair, dislodging the little white flower, which fell unnoticed to the floor. For no reason she could explain, she didn't want to see anyone, so she crept quietly down the stairs and found herself in the hall. It was empty, but there were voices coming from the common room.

" . . . told them they could have it for tonight. She was that close to fainting. They said they'd be on their way tomorrow, but I doubt that."

She recognized Greenie's voice, and briefly considered making herself known to assure her that they would indeed be leaving tomorrow, but before she could move another, deeper voice spoke.   A man.

"Where are they now?"

Greenie: "I gave them the room you know about. The only one left, and you can make of that what you will. She's in bed asleep and he's gone to fetch their luggage. I shouldn't wonder but she'd sleep most of the day. He told me he owed her a good meal. Said they'd be here for dinner."

The man's voice came again. "They'll be here for more than dinner. It's almost Midsummer. There was a pause. "You know what that means."

"Of course I know it, same as you do. "

"Is that why they're here?"

"Well that's the question, isn't it? The answer's not up to us. There's no knowing what will happen until it happens. We can't interfere. Watch and wait," said Greenie, "That's all we can do."

The conversation made Kath vaguely uneasy, and she found her own furtive eavesdropping distasteful. She opened the door as noiselessly as possible and stepped out into the day. She did not hear when a few moments later someone said goodbye to Greenie and slid out the door behind her, closing it softly and quietly.

The car park was empty. Without any clear intention she crossed the road, passing out of sunlight into the thin shadow of the trees. The wood was not as deep as she thought, just a narrow belt. Crossing it brought her to the edge, a sheer drop to a where the waves dashed against the cliffs. A little way out, two or three fishing-boats were rocking with the waves. Above them a gull wove invisible spider threads across the air. An onshore wind was blowing, driving clouds across a watercolor sky and rippling their shadows over the water.

Kath felt the wind against her body as a living force, and she had to brace herself to stand upright. Some distance to her left the cliff swung sharply inward, its curve framing a scrap of beach backed by woods and a rising hollow that must lead up to the road at the top. *Like the way down to Sea Cottage. Was it just last night we were there? That road we drove last night follows these cliffs. How many little coves like Elly's are tucked into these cliffs? Mick was certainly right about the place being remote.*

On either side of her the cliffs faced the sea in a series of sweeping curves and hollows that arced away on either hand, headland after headland as far as she could see. Beyond the cliffs the sea stretched to the horizon, an endless expanse of green shading to dark blue and then black. The surface heaved and shrugged like a live thing, and the boats on the water tossed like wood chips. From one of the boats a fisherman saw her and waved a greeting. She waved back. A sudden urge to go down to the water possessed her. She wanted to stand on the shifting edge where land and sea exchanged places, where minute frilled and faery creatures sported in the rocky tide pools. The waves would crash and hiss, and the water would run up the sand with deliberate haste and then drain back again to make way for the next wave. Without hesitation she turned back into the woods and through them out to the road. There was no traffic, and she saw no other buildings, no houses, nothing to mark any human habitation. Only the sun and the road and the belt of trees. The remote but ever-present sound of the waves coming in and coming in led her into a waking dream suspended between sea and sky. Time faded and there was only the present moment.

She had no idea how long she had been walking when she abruptly turned to the right, off the road and into the trees. *Now how did I know to do that?* The question came and was forgotten. In less than a minute she came to the little clearing where Mick had parked the car. *Okay, then, the path through the ravine down to the sea must be around here somewhere.* There it was at her feet, faint and fragile as an animal path, leading down. A moment later she was descending in daylight what she and Mick had blundered along in darkness the night before. On either side the rock walls rose steadily until they were over her head. Stubborn, twisted trees clung to the edges of the path and refused to give ground to the cliffs that grudged their growth. There was a sound of running water on her left, and now she could see, leaping headlong over rocks in its descent, the shallow stream that paralleled the path.

The emergence from the ravine to the sea was as abrupt in daylight as it had been in last night's moon-dusk, a sudden, unlooked-for transition from one world into another. Standing on the little shelf above the water she had a clear view out the v-shaped cove to the sea. In the middle distance a rock formation rose like a lopsided letter "n" whose center, a hollow gateway, had been carved out and cut through by the sea in some long past eon. Waves surged against the legs and boiled and sucked around the opening. The natural hypnotism of moving water held her, and how long she stood there she had no idea.

She reminded herself that somebody lived in this cove, somebody whose house she had visited, but who might not welcome un-invited exploration. This was private property. She might very well be trespassing. *Better mind my manners*, thought Kath, *and pay a duty call.* She headed up the beach to the little faery cottage, remembering that she had thought of it as the back door to Elfland. As she approached the ledge where the cottage stood, her footsteps slowed and stopped. There was no cottage. She stared in blank disbelief. The rocky ledge was innocent of any sign of a dwelling. *Now wait a minute*, she thought. And then in frustration and protest: *this is a little too much. First the car. Now the cottage? But there's no place to get lost here, no place for a whole house to hide, even a cottage as small as that one; there are no trees or underbrush, no crooked paths to cause confusion.*

Like a child looking for a lost toy, she paced the ledge, criss-crossing her own tracks in a fruitless effort to re-establish her memory. The path behind the ledge wound up between tall cliffs, everything was as she recalled it from last night. Only the little cottage was gone, as if it had never been. *This is crazy*, she told herself. *It was here. I was here last night. There were a lot of people, we drank tea, we heard stories. Mick was with me.* She looked about her. Then she walked deliberately over to what she still thought of as the cottage end, and stared at it fixedly, wanting to conjure out of blank space. *Right there is where the chimney was, she thought; right where I'm standing is the ghost of the hearth where Lame Elly sat. And there is nothing here. Nothing at all.* "Seeing things," she muttered. "I'm going crazy," followed immediately by, "No. I'm not crazy. I'm just tired." It sounded good, so she said it again, carefully enunciating each word. "I am not crazy. I am just tired." She followed up with another safe conclusion. "I'm probably just on the wrong beach." Clinging to that idea like a shipwrecked mariner to a lifesaver, she took it with her as she began the climb back up the path to the road, toward Mick and common sense and a real bed that she could really get into. She felt drained, emptied of experience by a fatigue so complete it bleached the world of color.

In that exhaustion the path seemed mountain-steep, every forward step she took dragged at her feet, opposed by something pulling her back. She grasped for a tree branch to help herself, and her outstretched hand caught in the ancient, thorny growth that mantled the cliff just at that place. A sharp pain in a finger made her pull back her hand and suck at the thorn-prick, but not before her fingers had touched a memory in the stone. She recalled the near-identical incident of the night before. *That's twice,* she thought. *But this is not the same path. Or is it?* She ran her fingers lightly, questioningly over the curves in the stone.

"They're from the long ago time," said a voice behind her.

Tiernon and Elly

She jumped at the sound. Surely no one could have come down the path, or up it for that matter, without her hearing. She turned, one hand still pressed against the rock. A man was standing in the path just below her. She recognized him. The man in the green jacket whose gaze had so unsettled her at the gab. His appearance now was equally unsettling. Had he risen out of the sea? His presence now was so ordinary, so solid and present that she began to doubt her own experience, the disappearance of the cottage, her bewildered search, the hallucinatory visions. Maybe they had all been pure imagination, some sort of hypnotic dream-trance from which she now was awakened. She put her hand on the stone, feeling for reality. It was hard, cool, smooth. It was there.

"I'm sorry," he said. "I didn't go to scare you. I recognized you from the gab, and saw you looking at the marks. Is it just chance you found them?"

"Yes," she said, "Just chance. I wasn't looking for anything. But they look like something I've seen before. Do you know who put them there? You said they were from the long ago time. How long ago was that?"

"A tidy way back. When the sun was young. The story goes that the stone folk cut them into the rock. They lived in the woods hereabouts and had a big firepit down the beach where they did their dances. We've found bones deep in the sand. Sometimes a storm will wash them out, but they fall apart when we try to pick them up."

Kath gave up trying to make any sense of what was happening. It was hard enough just trying to follow what he was saying. *The stone people. Trolls? Giants? Stone Age people? Was this folklore or history? Did this man even know the difference?* She wanted to know more about Elly, who lived so isolated, so confined a life, yet who could hold a crowd spellbound as she had last

night. *I shouldn't tread on Mick's turf, she thought. This is really his bailiwick; I'm just along for the ride. Still, no harm in asking.* "The woman who told that story last night about the . . the Grally Tus —
. . ."

His whole demeanor changed in an instant, and he interrupted as sternly as a parent to a child who should know better. "Don't say that name."

The intensity of his voice seemed to charge the atmosphere around them. The sun had gone behind clouds again, and the air that whispered across the back of her neck felt chill. She stared, dumbfounded.

"Some names have power," he told her, quieter now, but still insistent. "It's not a good idea to say them aloud. Especially not out of doors. You don't want to call . . . anything. Best not to tell it where you are."

He was quite serious, she saw with surprise. She remembered her conversation with Mick the night before, their casual discussion of the name Grally, its meaning and implications. She recalled the huge thing rushing through the woods, staring at her through the trees. *Did we call it?* she wondered. *Did I tell it where I was when I threw the stone?* She shivered. A puff of wind flipped all the leaves upside down, making the stone walls silver-green. The man was looking at her intently, and she couldn't tell whether he was fearful of the broken taboo or of having startled her.

"I won't say it again," she said quietly. "I'm sorry. I don't know your customs. I'm not from around here."

"No," he said, more easily now. "I could tell that last night."

Now why should that challenge her? But it did. "Oh? How could you tell?"

"Well, to start with, we knew he'd be coming, your friend who likes stories. And then, you know, it's not that big a place we live in. Everyone knows everyone else. Easy enough to spot a stranger. But mostly it was the way you listened, like it was some foreign speech we were talking."

"I didn't!" But she remembered that indeed, she had.

"And the way you looked around at us all, like we were in cages."

Not about to be put down by some country cousin, Kath struck back. Politely. "But you did that to us too. When we came in, you looked at us like we were some kind of new animal."

"Ah, that's different. You were the strangers. This is our place, not yours. It's us that have to look you over and find out who you are."

Now she was really nettled. "Well, you looked me over. Did you find out who I am?"

He was unperturbed. "She did. Elly. She knows who you are. That's the reason she asked you back."

"Oh, is it now?" She tilted her head and looked at him with just the hint of challenge. *All right, smarty, answer this one.* "Well then, who am I?"

"Don't you know, then?"

He was not being rude. He had simply taken her literally, turning her question back on her. The air crackled with challenge like a sudden electric charge.

Does anybody know who they are, really? she thought. She forced herself to breathe deep, go slow, think before speaking, aware that a balance she had not even been aware of had unexpectedly shifted. The conversation had tilted away from polite chance-meeting talk into something much deeper and realer, something with an undercurrent whose tug she could feel but not identify. He was in charge now, this stranger she hadn't expected to meet.

She was determined to take back the conversation, willfully to misunderstand the meaning of his question. "I'm sorry. I should have introduced myself. My name's Kath." She waited. He simply looked at her. "And yours is?"

"I'm Tiernon," he said.

Like I should know who that is, thought Kath. "I was glad the . . . glad Elly asked me back. I'd like to see her again."

"That's why I'm here, to bring you. She saw you coming."

Something beyond Kath's imagining was moving and carrying her with it. She had a giddy sense of letting go, surrendering her will to some larger force, spiraling down a winding wind, blown by it and yet part of it. She enjoyed the sensation. "Right now, you mean? She did ask me back, I just didn't think it would be so soon. But how could she know I'd be coming when I didn't know myself until I got here? I was just out for a walk and . . . "

His voice cut across her protest. "She knew."

She gave up trying to grasp the strangeness of what was happening, let alone any meaning it might contain. "Well then, let's go," said Kath.

He turned at once, and went down the path with the gait of one who knew in his bones every turn. She followed more slowly, on the lookout for roots and stones.

They came out of shadows onto the little shelf. The sun was westering, its level light hitting the cliffs straight on, sending a golden light over the little landscape and throwing every contour into sharp relief. Out on the water the fishing boats were turning homeward. On the beach a few yards from the rock where she had sat a small boat was pulled up and overturned. Lame Elly's cottage stood solid and firm and real on its ledge. From the chimney smoke was rising.

"She's here, Elly," her companion announced. "I found her halfway up the path. She was looking at the mazes."

Kath halted in the doorway, her eyes sun-dazzled so that the interior was hidden in formless blackness for a moment.

"Thank you, Tiernon." Lame Elly's voice was lower than Kath remembered, pitched now for conversation, not storytelling. In her rocking chair next to the fire, she might not have moved since last night, her hands busy with knitting. She turned her blind gaze toward the doorway. "Come in, my dear, come in. I can't get up to greet you, but you're very welcome. Come sit here by the fire. Tiernon, get her the chair. That's right. And you can make tea before you go."

Kath's eyes were getting used to the dimness of indoors, and as they adapted she looked around her. The cottage appeared smaller than when crowded with people. The bed which last night had sagged under the weight of too many bodies now was neatly made, a thin blanket folded at the foot. A wooden shelf pegged to the wall held cups and bowls, and little cutouts in the edge dangled spoons ready for use. The table, bare except for a cracked jug holding a sheaf of ferns, was pushed against the wall opposite the fire. But it was real, it was there, like everything else in the cottage. She felt her mind tipping with the chair.

We daren't go a-hunting.

Oh yes we do.

Still blinking from the sun, Kath allowed herself to be settled in the chair he brought. It was straight-backed and rickety, and she found that she had to perch carefully to keep it from tipping. Whatever imp of the perverse was playing tricks with her memory and perception obviously didn't do things by halves. She felt her grip on reality slackening, the solid world dissolving like mist in sunlight. Her mind started spinning on itself like a reel at the end of a thread, and she suppressed a near-hysterical laugh, picturing herself as the witness in some otherworld detective story: "The Case of the Slackening Grip." *'And where was this Grip when you last saw it, miss? It was right here, Inspector, right where you're standing. All right, men; fan out and search the premises. We're looking for a Grip on Reality. It can't have gone far; there hasn't been enough time.'* *And that will be enough of that,* she told herself. *Pull yourself together, Kath.* But the Inspector's face haunted her, though she couldn't place it.

Elly's face was turned toward Kath. "It's a quiet welcome you'll get here, I'm afraid. 'A house with no dog, with no cat, with no baby: a house without laughter.' That's what we say hereabouts."

Kath felt she ought to cap the proverb with one of her own, but she had none handy, so she simply said, "I don't mind. I like the quiet."

"Looking at the spirals, were you?"

The knitting needles clicked in quiet rhythm, the yarn went looping in and out.

"Yes," said Kath.

"And you've seen them before." It was a statement, not a question.

"Yes, I'm sure I have. Somewhere or other. In a book or something, I suppose. They look awfully familiar."

"In a book, you say? Oh, I shouldn't think so. What would they be doing in a book?"

"I meant in a photograph in a . . . a history book, or a tourist guide or something like that. If they're so old they must be like . . . like other rock carvings and cave paintings that . . . that you hear about. Something famous. They must be well-known." She floundered lamely to a halt, the words sounding fatuous and inane in her own ears.

"Well now that depends on what you mean by well-known. Folks hereabouts know them. And it seems you know them too, but certainly not from a photograph, I should think. Thank you Tiernon, I'll drink it in a minute, just set it on the stool there."

Letting her knitting dangle, Elly reached with one hand for the cup that Tiernon had set beside her chair, not gropingly, as one newly blind and lost in darkness, but with gentle touch, sure of her range.

She's been blind a long time, thought Kath. *She's at peace with it.*

The cup Tiernon handed Kath might have been the same one she drank from last night, cracked, with a chip in the rim and the handle broken off. And the tea in it was just as scalding. Elly's hand was curled round her own mug, cradling it for warmth before she set it on the stool again. Kath wondered briefly if everyone's hands but hers were lined with asbestos. The needles resumed their clicking as Elly continued.

"Yes, they're old, those spirals. They're the oldest of anything I know that's a made thing. But the sun has to shine on them just right. And you have to know just where to look. My grandmother told me, as her grandmother told her, and hers before her, the story about how they came to be there. Will you like to hear it?"

"Yes," said Kath. "Very much," simultaneously thinking *Wow, what Mick would give for a chance like this. Too bad it's me and not him.* She took a long swallow of tea and settled as comfortably as she could on the hard, teetering chair as Elly began her story.

"*Back when the sun was young and the sea was not much older, a woman was walking on the shore. She was of Elverie, and . . .*"

Elverie. The strange word caught at Kath, but the story was going on and . . .

"*. . . the way you would know it was this. There was never a print of her foot in the sand or a shadow falling before or behind her though the sun was shining. Nary a sign of her passage, though you could see the shape of her plain enough. Wherever she stepped . . .*"

The cottage was gone. She was standing on the rocky ledge in the morning of the world. She was on an empty shore with nothing to companion her except the sea in her eyes and the sun on her head and the wind that tugged at her hair. As she had done a hundred times, as she would always do, she took the side path down to the beach, skirting the embers of last night's fire. Under her bare feet the sand was wet and cool. Swags of seaweed lay along the water's edge where the retreating waves had left them. There was no sound. No wind brushed her ears, no bird cried, no wave shushed, not even the rustle of sedge-grass tickled the quiet. But behind the hush was the music of a sea-cave and its rock walls were strummed by the waves that surged and played within it. The music called and she followed. Directly in front of her was a high rock wall and carved into the wall was the spiral and the spiral was the wall. It was flat against the rock, yet it led inward. She passed within the narrow opening with the sun behind her and began to tread the spiral, while watching her shadow as it dodged and darted ahead or to one side or the other, feeling it disappear behind her. And all the while the sea-cave sang into the silence. All was in shadow but looking down she could see her feet as they trod her shadow underfoot, one foot after the other foot after the other and her whole being followed her feet. Soon she could see nothing at all, but she knew she was still moving, winding, turning and returning, tracing and retracing the labyrinth that was the turning skies and the sea's deep currents and the circling of her blood. Then the song of the sea-cave was a pounding in her body like great waves dashing and dashing against the arch of rock, and she knew as she came nearer to the center that she was close to the thing she was looking for and that in the next minute she would find it.

"And when she come back," said Elly, "she put the story of her journey on the cliff wall. Traced it right into the stone with her finger, she did. And when her daughter was born the first thing she did was carry her up the path and show her.

"And that daughter showed her daughter, and so it has come, mother to daughter, mother to daughter all down the years. The tale will run to chase the sun."

The story was over and the golden light of late afternoon slanted through the window.

"Your tea will be getting cold," said Lame Elly. "Tiernon, bring her a fresh cup."

A mug of fresh hot tea appeared in her hand and she drank a long swallow. Then she heard her own voice coming from a long way off.

"Mother to daughter. Then you must have showed your daughter."

"Aye, I did. But she died when Tiernon was born. So the chain was broken."

Kath wanted to respond, but the room was swinging around her in slow circles and she grabbed onto the seat of her chair to keep it still. *Too much caffeine, that's what's wrong with me,* thought Kath. Things were happening too fast. Suddenly she wanted Mick. She wanted his sturdy common sense and his plain world of every day.

"Somebody's coming down the path," said Tiernon.

Mick

Running footsteps sounded on the ledge and someone was beating a rapid tattoo on the door. It swung open and Mick stood in the doorway, breathless and disheveled.

"I'm looking for—" He broke off as he saw her. "Kath! You're here. Thank heaven. Somebody said—"

"You're the young man from last night," said Elly, her sightless gaze passing over him like a benediction. "Come in and be welcome. We've been having a nice visit. What did somebody say?"

He hardly heard her; he was talking to Kath.

"I got back with the bags and you weren't there. And I couldn't find you anywhere. Somebody said they'd seen a woman up on the cliffs, and I was afraid . . . I thought maybe you'd — there's no guard rail up there — you'd walk right off the edge of the world and not even know it. "

"Oh Mick, I'm sorry." As long as she hung onto the chair, she was relatively solid, and it was imperative that Mick not see how unsteady she felt or how the room rocked and tilted around her. "I had no idea you'd worry. I couldn't sleep, so I went for a walk."

"A walk! You're miles from the inn. How the hell could you walk all this way?"

"It didn't seem to take very long. Besides, I didn't think you'd be back so soon."

"So soon!" His voice rose, anxiety and relief giving way to anger. "Do you know what time it is?" He was almost shouting.

"No, I don't know. What time is it? Is it late?"

"Is it late!" Now he was shouting. "It's six o'clock in the evening! You've been gone all day! I left you in bed at nine o'clock this morning. I got back with the luggage thinking you'd still be asleep, and the bed's empty, the room's empty, Greenie doesn't know where you are, she never even saw you leave. I went out to the edge of the cliffs, and the wind almost blew me off. You could at least have left a note before you started wandering all over the place."

"I'm sorry, Mick, truly I am. I didn't think of a note because I never meant to be gone long. I never thought you'd worry."

"You never thought I'd worry! You never thought period! Of course I'd worry!" Belatedly Mick became conscious that there were other people in the room. He brought his voice down to conversation level and turned to Lame Elly, steadily knitting. "I apologize for barging in like this, for making all this noise. I . . . I was worried about Kath."

"No apology needed, but now you're here, you'd better look after her. She needs tending."

"I don't need tending," said Kath to the world, "I'm perfectly fine."

But the words would not come out, and the chair started to rock under her, and then it tipped. She was aware of Mick reaching to catch her, of a voice—but whose it was she didn't know—saying, "She's been ill, hasn't she?"

Then she fell through earth and sea into the maze and the floor came up to meet her and dunted her hard on the head.

The voice reached her across great distance, down the tunnel from another world. "She's coming around."

She opened her eyes to a row of anxious faces looking down at her: Mick, Greenie, the man Tiernon. Only one mattered. He was holding her hand, she realized.

"Mick?"

"Right beside you, Kath." His hand was warm, cradling hers.

"What happened?"

"You fainted. You were down at the cottage with Lame Elly and you passed out cold."

I didn't, she thought indignantly. *Women don't faint these days. That's old fashioned.* But she didn't say it. What she said was, "I'm not there now. Where am I?"

"You're back at The Wicken Tree, the inn where we had breakfast. You're in the room. Our room."

"I don't remember going to bed."

"I should think you didn't remember. You were out like a light. Tiernon and I carried you up the path from the cottage, and a devil of a time we had, too. Next time I'll bring ropes. We put you in the car and drove you back here and Greenie put you right to bed."

"How long ago was that?"

"About an hour ago. You had me scared, Kath, it took you so long to come around. That was a nasty knock on the head. You're going to have a bruise on your temple where you hit the floor. A real shiner. How are you feeling now?"

"Okay, I think. Well, kind of shaky. . . . Mick?"

She was whispering, and he leaned his head down to hear.

"Send them away."

He nodded, and turned to the others. "She wants to rest. I'll stay with her."

With quick understanding Greenie took Tiernon by the arm and steered him out the door. "We'll be in the bar. I've got customers to see to. If she needs anything, just call down the stairs."

The room was quiet when they had gone. Mick was still holding her hand.

"Anything you need? Some water? Tea? Coffee?"

She smiled weakly and shook her head.

"No tea or coffee, thank you. I've had enough. But there's something I would like."

"Yes?"

"You."

"I'm right here."

"Could you . . . come closer?"

"Closer how? You mean get in bed?"

She nodded.

"Anything to please the lady." He shucked shirt and pants and slid in beside her.

"Closer."

"Like this?" He slipped an arm under her head.

"Closer." Insistent.

"Kath, my dear idiot, you need to lie quiet. You're so tired and worn-out you're punchy. You're hurt and sick. You don't know what you want."

"Yes I do."

He rose on one elbow, looking worriedly down at her.

"Closer." Softly now.

Lightly, lightly, afraid to break her, he touched her cheek, ran a finger along the line of her jaw, traced the curve under her ear. He kissed the tip of her nose, the corner of her mouth, the hollow at the base of her throat where her heartbeat fluttered, then turned to cover and hold her as she rose to meet him. Expecting at most some gentle moments of sleepy pleasure before she dropped off as she surely must, he was unprepared for the fierceness with which she met and returned his caresses, the primal abandon with which she opened herself to him and took him in, guiding and leading the dance as they spiraled in and down and up and up. He surrendered to her passion, never suspecting that he was a surrogate, never thinking that his lovemaking could be the substitute for a longed-for, never until now suspected, other experience. Afterward they lay side by side, strangely shy after the storm.

"You asleep?" He spoke softly.

"Mmmmn, not quite . . . half, maybe." Her voice was blurry with sleep and he thought she had dropped off. Then, "Mick?"

"Yes?"

"The Grally Whatsitsname . . . ." The murmur was so soft he had to bend to hear her.

"What about him?"

"Don't ask any questions."

He thought at first she was joking. "Ah ha. Turning the tables, are we? Giving Mick a

115

taste of his own medicine. 'Ask no questions, mind your manners, listen quietly.'"

"No, I'm serious: don't ask about him. Don't say the name."

"Why not?"

"You'll spook the horses."

"What horses?"

"The people around here."

"How do you know?"

"He told me. That guy, Tiernon. I said the name out loud and he freaked. Wouldn't even let me finish. It's . . . if you say his name in daylight, you call him. At night he's only in the story."

He waited for her to tell him why, and when she didn't he saw that she was asleep, deep in the total, undefended surrender of a very young child.

Carefully, so as not to wake her, he slid out of bed, took his clothes, switched off the lamp and tiptoed out of the room. In the hall bathroom he dressed quickly, then went downstairs.

Stories

The big common room, part bar and part dining-room, had a scattering of customers now, regulars stopping by for a pint before supper, sunburned summer people in search of food after a hard day's play. Tiernon was sitting at a little table by the front window. Mick went over to him.

"May I join you?"

Tiernon nodded and gestured to the chair across from him. "Asleep, is she?"

"Out like a light. Good thing, too. She's had a pretty rough couple of days."

"Elly said she needed tending."

"Elly had it right. She and Elly seem to get along."

"Seem to. Elly could tell she liked the stories."

"Yes, the stories. Elly has a lot of them, doesn't she?"

"Enough."

"You must know a few yourself. I guess you've heard them all your life?"

"Everyone around here has stories, you hear them all the time. They're just the way things are."

"Like history, sort of?"

Tiernon shrugged. "What's history? That's just what's written down by somebody who wasn't there."

Not bad, thought Mick. *Sharper than I expected.* Cautiously, he ventured to take it further.

"But you weren't there, were you, for those stories we heard last night?"

"Not myself, no, but there's folks around who were, or they know somebody who was, or remember where something happened and can point to it."

"Is that important: where something happened? Must you always be able to point to it? Don't most stories make up their own 'where'?"

"That's daft, making things up. Don't need to do that when they're already there."

"But that one last night that Elly told about the—" Tiernon's sudden tensing reminded him what Kath had said, and he skirted the precipice. "—about the castle and the three sons?" He saw Tiernon relax, and went on carefully. "I mean, there aren't any castles around here, are there?"

"Not now, there's not. That's why we have the stories, to keep in rememberment what's gone before."

"You mean there was a castle once? Up on the cliffs? Somewhere in the wood?"

Tiernon was patient, as with a child. "For sure there was, or there wouldn't be a story about it, now would there? But the land changes. Sometimes the sea rises and covers the shore. Sometimes the cliffs fall and the sea swallows them. The sea eats the land. It's always hungry."

Mick's mind sorted through all the "drowned land" stories he'd read: Atlantis and Lyonesse and Ys, the Lady of the Lake, the Lands Under the Wave. Maybe there was something there. *Interesting image, a ruined castle under the sea. No reason why there couldn't be one.*

But if there had been a castle then there must also have been a Grally Tusker, or some beast for which that was the name.

In the pause in the conversation the background noises in the room surged forward to fill the vacuum: the clink of glasses, the clatter of silverware on plates, the kitchen door banging. The television behind the bar was droning out the local weather report: "partly cloudy, sudden squalls, small craft warnings." A couple of young male voices were raised in song. A woman laughed. The soft, shrill voice of a very young child cut the smoky air. Snatches of other conversations wove a lattice of sound. ". . . up early in the morning . . ." — "can't get them to bed at all when it's this light" — "almost had him in the boat, but then at the last minute . . . " — "told you you'd get sunburned if you didn't wear a hat . . ." — "be here for the Solstice celebration . . . " — "wouldn't miss it for the world. That's why we came."

A nearer voice cut in. "Take your order? You must be ready for a hot meal after all that to-do. And how is your young lady?" It was Greenie, voluble, efficient, poised with pad and pencil.

"She's sound asleep," said Mick.

"Ah, well, that's what she needs. Sleep the night through, she'll be a different woman tomorrow. She's lovely, your lady. Like the girl in the story. These old stories have some truth in them, don't they?" She looked from him to Tiernon and back again. "Will you be staying on, then?"

"Looks like it," said Mick. "If we can keep the room for a few more days?"

"Keep it and welcome. Remind me to have you sign the Visitor's Book. It's on the big dresser in the entrance hall. And then you'll be here for Midsummer Eve."

"Ah, that's a special time, isn't it?" asked Mick. "Do you have a solstice celebration?"

"Tiernon here is the one to ask. He'll tell you all about it. Now, did you want to order?"

"What's on tonight?" asked Tiernon.

"A nice pot roast with noodles in onion gravy. Been cooking all afternoon. Or you could have a hot pie."

It was Mick's cue, and he looked at Tiernon a little diffidently. "I'd . . . uhm . . . like to stand you dinner if I may. I could never have got Kath back here without you. And I'm enjoying the conversation."

"So am I," said Tiernon, an answer Mick hadn't expected. "Happy to accept the invitation, but mine's on the house. Thanks anyway."

"Well, then. Order up."

"I'll have the pot roast," he told the waiting Greenie. "And a double order of noodles and gravy. Got any salad?"

"Nice fresh lettuce, love. Just out of the garden. And spring onions.

"That'll do."

Greenie turned to Mick.

"I'll have the pot roast too. And some of that salad."

When she had moved on, his impulse was to return to the conversation about stories. But the moment had died, and he felt it would have been awkward to resurrect it. Better stick to safer topics.

Tiernon was watching him quietly, so he decided to ease into the conversation slowly. "What's this wicken tree the Inn's named after? I don't see any tree close nearby."

"Ah, there's a story there. There's only a stump left now, but years and years ago it was big enough to shade the front door. Part of a big wood that grew hereabout in the olden days.

The Wickenwood. And the Wicken Tree was right in the middle, so that's where they put the Inn, to be handy, see?"

Mick forebore to ask who "they" were. "Handy to what? To the tree? Why?"

"Folk used to say that the tree was a gateway, a passage between worlds. You could dream under it and the dream would take you there."

"Yes, I've heard that sort of thing before. Like the Eildon Tree in the Thomas Rhymer story."

"There's a power of stories like that. Where did you hear that one?"

"It's pretty well-known," said Mick, avoiding any mention of books or research. "And the Wicken Tree was like that?"

"It was, till some fellow chopped it down. Way before my time. It's supposed to keep growing back, but I've never seen it happen. The stump's still there, beside the front steps."

Now that the conversation was launched, Mick got down to his real interest.

"What's this celebration everyone's talking about? A special occasion. Private?"

"No, not most of it. Some, of course . . . " He let it trail away. "Midsummer Eve. Folk around here make a big thing of it. There'll be an outdoor party. A lot of food and drink."

"Like a Harvest Festival, is it?"

"No, not, not exactly." Tiernon was patient, but he clearly thought Mick impossibly ignorant.

Ignorance is its own reward, thought Mick. *Ignorance gets explanations*. "Go on," said Mick invitingly.

"Harvest celebrates having food to get through the dark time. The days are almost gone before they're here. No sun till almost midday and then just a few hours before it's dark again. That's when you pack the snow around your house to stop the wind, and sit by the fire."

"Then what is this one?"

Tiernon was patient. "It's Midsummer, y'see. Things growing. So there's the sun. And the bride."

"Bride? Is there a wedding?"

"Not a church wedding, no. But every year a girl gets chosen."

"An agriculture myth."

"You might call it that."

124

"Acting out the story? Fertility, matings of gods and mortals, that sort of thing?"

"We're trying to make this year special. Things haven't been so good, see, the past several years. Crops poor, fish scarce. We're hoping, if we do everything right, this year will turn it around. Start over."

"How will you do that?"

"Depends on whoever's this year's bride. It needs someone new, fresh energy."

"I see," said Mick. "To renew the promise. Folklore's full of stories like that."

"That what you call them? Stories? Did you never think they might really happen?"

There was a pause. Now what had he said to make this man so touchy? The phrase that he had translated to Kath as the meaning of gab came back to him: *where the stories are real*. It hadn't meant much at the time.

"You want to know more about our stories, you'd better come to the Midsummer Eve party. You could bring her."

They were back on safe ground.

"Kath? She'd love it. She really goes for things like that. Who directs the operation? Must be a big job."

"Everybody helps. There'll be a bonfire roast, Greenie'll send stuff from the kitchen, people will bring breads and pastries. Cider, beer, lifewater, things like that."

"But isn't anyone in charge of the festivities? No Master of the Revels?"

"If there is one, it's me. But a thing like this, been going on a long time around here. We all know what to do. Everybody has a part."

"Everybody? Even strangers? Guests?"

"They all fit in."

"Then I'll be sure to bring Kath."

"You do that. She'll fit right in."

Wandering

She was wandering in a wood. She was lost. She was Snow White running from the huntsman, and the knots in the trees were the eyes of owls staring at her. The fluttering leaves were the wings of bats wheeling and swooping across the face of the moon. The creakings of the branches were the cryings of ghosts. The brambles that caught at her were the grasping hands of lost and desperate creatures trying to hold her, trying to keep her from finding the car. She could see it through the trees, but the path wound endlessly, sometimes near, sometimes far. It turned and she turned with it, and she could see, through the trees, the gingerbread house.

　　　When she came close, it was Lame Elly's cottage, nestled against the cliff at one end of the ledge. She looked for the Inspector to tell him she had *found it, but as usual he wasn't there when she needed him. Walking toward the cottage, she was conscious of an almost palpable silence. The little house had the forlorn look that all deserted buildings have, a patient waiting for those who once were there to come back. She knew that no one was at home, that no one had been at home in that house for a very long time. Nevertheless, she knocked on the door. It swung back at her touch, and she looked inside.*

The room was empty. Sand and dead leaves gathered in the corners. The air was cold with the settled chill of a place long abandoned. Outside the waves whispered up the little beach, but the sound became wind in the trees, and she knew she was in a wood. She shivered.

Kath vs. Mick

Kath half-woke and turned uneasily, feeling for the reassurance of her own physical presence, the actuality of her body in the bed. Then the rustle of the covers became again the sound of wind in the trees, and she slid back into timelessness.

The door of the hut banged in the wind. Someone was knocking on the cottage door. The sound grew sharper, more insistent.

She opened her eyes.

There was Mick, standing in the doorway with a tray. The mingled smells of vegetable soup and fresh-baked bread brought her fully awake, telling her in no uncertain terms that she was ravenously hungry.

"Greenie says you're to eat this. All of it."

She pushed herself upright. "I'll eat, I promise. If you'll stay here and tell me what's been going on. I've been down the rabbit hole with Alice. What time is it? "

"It's three o'clock in the afternoon. You've been sleeping since last night."

"What day is it?"

He settled the tray on a pillow on her lap, and sat himself at the foot of the bed.

"It's tomorrow."

"Think you're smart, don't you?"

"Okay. It's the day after you got yourself lost and went wandering all over creation. I still don't know how you got that far that fast."

"I'm sorry, Mick. I've been a real nuisance. I'll behave myself from now on."

"How's your head?"

"Fine. Why shouldn't it be?"

"You took an awful knock yesterday. I told you you'd have a shiner, and you do. A beauty. Don't you remember?"

"No, not very much. But then I just woke up. I expect it'll all come back in a minute." She shook her head, trying to remember. Her eyes closed and her voice rose in a chant:

"Come if you will
but do none ill.
To act in trust
bring with you dust,
if you would free
the Dreaming Tree."

"Where did you hear that, Kath," asked Mick. "What's the Dreaming Tree?"

"I don't know," she said. "It's like something I heard in a dream a long time ago, and it just now came back, the way dreams can do."

"Forget the dream and get started on this soup. You're a couple of meals behind, and you still haven't had that dinner I promised you."

She broke off a hunk of bread, dipped it in the soup, and took a large bite. The crust was crisp and crunchable, and the melting richness of the soup on her tongue was a new enjoyment. Swallowing, she looked up at him.

"If it's tomorrow, what have you been doing all this time?"

"I had dinner last night with that guy Tiernon — I'm not sure I like him, but he's worth talking to — and then came upstairs here to be with you."

131

"You said I've been asleep for hours. What about you? Did you sleep?"

"Sure did."

She was working on another chunk of soup-dunked bread and trying without success to stop the drips from running down her chin. Mick blotted her with the napkin she had forgotten to unfold, then tucked it under her chin. There was a funny little pause in which they looked at one another, each of them wondering how to say to the other what needed to be said. Mick began it.

"Kath, I'm worried about you."

"Worried how?"

"Don't take this wrong. I think my asking you to come along on my little folk-finding expedition was a mistake. No, let me finish. I believe you're not well, or at least, not as well as you think you are. You haven't been taking care of yourself, and I haven't been taking care of you."

She wanted to respond, to share the weight of what was happening to her, had been happening over the last days. She had to unburden herself, at least get somebody else to help her deal with it. It was too much to carry alone. Afraid already of what Mick's response would be, she still had to try. How to begin?

"I don't take it wrong, and you're sweet to be concerned. But I love being here, and it wasn't a mistake to ask me. I'm quite well, really. All I needed was some sleep. But Mick, listen. Just listen, will you, and hear me out? I'm not sick, but I am *something*, and I don't quite know what. There are some things . . . Remember when we were sitting in the car and you were telling me about Lame Elly, how she was a great discovery and all? It was right after that that things started being — I don't know — weird. I could see right through you."

"You could always see through me, Kath."

"It's not a joke, Mick." She shook her head, and winced. "Ow! I guess you were right about my head. It hurts now, all right. No, I mean I could actually see through you. You were transparent. But I thought then that it was just that eerie light. Then we went to that gab thing. And I loved that. But I had the oddest feeling when she was telling the story." Kath picked at the coverlet, then took a deep breath and plunged. "It was all really happening right then, and it was happening to me. And afterward, when we got lost in the woods and couldn't find the car, I had the feeling that something was keeping us from finding it. We're not that stupid, and there wasn't enough of those woods to lose a car in. I still felt a bit like the . . . the monster in the story was waiting for me. Mick if you laugh at me . . ."

"I'm not laughing," said Mick.

"And then after that, when we decided to stay there until morning, I told you at first I heard an animal. But I was fudging; it wasn't an animal. Not an ordinary animal, anyway. I know you won't believe this, but it was the— "

He broke in. "The Grally Tusker. Well of course. What else would you expect? Between Elly's story and your imagination, it couldn't have been anything else. But you were asleep. I know you were. I saw you."

Her shoulders sagged. She should have known. "You think I was dreaming. How can I convince you that I wasn't? I could smell the woods, hear the underbrush moving, feel the hard, lumpy ground with sticks and twigs digging into my back. If I was dreaming then, I'm dreaming now, because everything — this room, the bread and soup, even you — is no more real than what happened that night." Her voice rose in ascending scale and broke off in a little angry laugh.

Something serious is going on here, thought Mick. *She's angry, but more than angry, she's frightened. Very frightened.* She looked so desperate and yet so defiant, that he had all he could do not to gather her in his arms. He wanted to gentle her and reassure her, as you might a child. But she wasn't a child, and she wouldn't take kindly to being stroked and petted. He had to go carefully. "Well, I'm certainly real," he said mildly. "We can agree on that. But if you weren't dreaming, what do you think was happening?"

"I think I was still in it, still part of the story. I think in a way I still am. No, wait, let me go on. Because everything that happened after that, everything that I know was real — waking up and finding the car and coming here and having breakfast — all that begins to feel like a dream. It all starts swirling around, like when you try to remember a dream and the harder you try the faster you lose it. Can you fill me in?"

"Not much, and I'm just as confused as you are. I left you in bed at the inn and found you at Lame Elly's cottage, pale as a ghost and hanging on to the furniture. Then you keeled over, and Tiernon and I brought you back and put you to bed. Whatever happened in between, you'll have to tell me."

"I'm not sure I know."

"What do you mean you're not sure?"

"I'm starting to remember, but it's all swirling around, like I said. Or else . . . or else it isn't swirling and something very strange is going on."

"How do you mean, 'strange'?"

"Well, this morning—no, yesterday morning after you left—I woke up, and everything was normal again. I mean, I was right here, not in any story or anything. I knew where I was and who I was. But when I went out on the cliffs—I don't know how to say it— everything was different. And I saw . . . " *No, better not tell him that.* She skipped quickly on. "I was in a different time. But it was a time I remembered. I'd been there before . . . " She broke off. "I know it sounds crazy, but it isn't." She looked at him anxiously.

"It doesn't sound crazy."

She loved him for that. But then he went on, and spoiled it.

"But it does sound like the aftermath of real illness. No, you listen to me now. I've been counting up, and before you fell asleep last night, to my certain knowledge you'd had in about thirty-six hours exactly one and a half pieces of toast, heaven only knows how much tea and coffee, and zero sleep. All these symptoms you're describing, dreams seeming real and reality seeming like a dream — I'd be willing to bet they're the result of illness combined with extreme hunger and sleep deprivation. You've been spacing out. Hallucinating. Having waking dreams. It's nothing to worry about, and you'll get over it as soon as you get rested and fed. Which I intend to make sure happens."

He would, too. All that was most endearing and most frustrating about Mick: his protective concern for her coupled with his certainty that she couldn't take care of herself; his rational mind—that found a reasonable explanation for everything—was building a wall between them nearly impossible to breach. But she had to try.

"Mick, please try to listen and hear me. I was not having dreams, and I was not hallucinating. Whatever has been going on—

and I don't know what that is — was not a dream, waking or sleeping. I just now woke up from a dream, and it was about you, and I know perfectly well it was a dream. I could tell you all about it and still know that it was a dream. This wasn't like that. And there's another thing . . . " She hesitated, then went on. "Yesterday, on the path to the cove where we went that first night . . . I looked again at those carvings. They're spirals carved into the rock face, very old, prehistoric I think. They're not dreams; they're absolutely real, they're still there. You can go and see for yourself. But Mick, here's the thing. The minute I saw them I recognized them. I'd seen them before." She waited warily for his response, knowing already what it was likely to be. It was.

"Kath, I don't doubt for a minute that those carvings are real. And I'd like to see them again in full daylight. You can show them to me when you're feeling better. But I'm pretty sure I know what was going on with you when you thought you recognized them. *Déjà vu.* It isn't paranormal or spooky or psychic or anything like that. It's a perfectly natural phenomenon everybody has at some time or other. It's nothing but a chemical process in the brain that registers the same impression twice within milliseconds. You had seen them before — only it was just seconds before. That's all."

He was being perfectly reasonable, and he was making perfect sense. How could she get him to see that making sense was not the point, that she was entirely well and entirely rational, and that she needed desperately for him to understand and believe her? Before she could say anything, he went on.

"Tell you what. If you'll promise me that you'll be good and do as you're told — which means staying in bed for now, resting up and eating — I'll promise you a treat. Think you might be ready for some fun? There's going to be a party tomorrow night, and we're invited. More than that, you are specially invited. By our pal Tiernon. Now, about eating regular. You have to make up for lost meals. Could you eat another bowl of soup? You sure put away the first one pretty fast. And the bread too."

So that was that. The subject was closed. She knew better than to try to re-open it, at least for the moment. Maybe if she cooperated, ate properly, got enough sleep, did whatever was needed to "be good," they would both be readier to talk and listen to each other later on.

"I guess I could have some more soup, if it came with some more of that good bread for dunking. But about this party — whose party is it? If this is such an out-of-the-way place, who would come to a party?"

"There are people up here. Just not very many. Don't forget about Great Wicken. And Little Wicken. They may seem small to us. But not to themselves. This party seems to be a sort of community affair. It's an annual event, I gather. A Solstice celebration. Midsummer. Also probably a way for the locals to earn a bit of extra cash."

"And how am I 'specially invited'?"

"Tiernon told me to bring you. His exact words were, 'we'll fit her in.'"

"That's a strange way of inviting a person. Fit me in to what? Does he think I'm some sort of oddball that people have to make allowances for?"

"Don't get riled. He didn't mean it that way. It's just how it came up in conversation."

"Okay, okay. I guess I could use a little fun. But I'm still awfully tired. And you're right about my head. It does hurt. Like the mischief."

Which was true. Her head had begun to ache ferociously, and she felt curiously heavy and leaden-limbed, like trying to run under water. More sleep was definitely not a bad idea. If only she did not dream. As soon as Mick left with the tray she relaxed back on the pillows and her eyes closed of their own accord.

When he returned with the second bowl of soup, she was sound asleep and breathing in easy rhythm. He did not try to wake her.

Waking Dreams

Hours later, Kath woke to darkness and a silence made deeper by the faint whisper beside her of Mick's even breathing. A little breeze from the open window stirred the night air. All around her was the luminous northern night and the profound, sensuous quiet of a world without traffic. She lay wrapped in silence. Somewhere far off a dog barked; then all was still again.

Out of the quiet, and faint in the distance, a noise began, the sound of some large animal crashing through the underbrush. As in her night in the woods, it seemed to be coming closer.

And I am awake, for sure this time, she told herself. She thought of waking Mick to enlist him as a witness, to prove to him that there was no possibility of hallucination, but decided against it. *I don't need Mick to tell me when I'm awake. Or to protect me. I'm indoors where the roof and walls will keep me safe. Nothing can get at me. I can even say the name if I want.* She mouthed it silently to herself: *Grally Tusker.* It tasted faintly rank, old and savage in the back of her throat. As the syllables whispered across her tongue, the crashing got louder. Almost immediately, running human footsteps sounded beneath her open window, then stopped. There was an ominous silence. Then something came exploding out of the wood. Whatever it was, it, too, stopped.

Then there was more silence.

She had to find out. Slipping out of bed, Kath crossed to the window and leaned out, her hands propped on the sill, looking out the window into the strange northern twilight.

At first she had no reaction at all, not even astonishment. It was not so much what she saw as what she didn't see that was so unexpected. Nothing was there. There was no evidence of anyone or anything that might have caused the noises she had so clearly heard. But that absence was dwarfed by the larger absence of all that should have been there, that had been there when last she looked. There were no tidy flowerbeds, no gravel car park, no road, no farther woods. A field of grass, its green dimmed to grey in the colorless light, stretched as far as she could see on either side, mounding into low, treeless hills, and halted abruptly in the middle distance ahead by the invisible knife edge of the cliffs. The night wind siffled in the grasses all around her, otherwise there was no sound.

There was no transition. The grass felt cool and springy under her bare feet. She looked back toward the inn for reassurance. It was not there. There was only grass in every direction. And then she knew, as she had known out on the cliffs, that she was looking at the world not in what had been her present moment, but in a time so long ago that time itself had no meaning. The wind ruffled her hair, and the air smelled new and clean and cold. She was rather enjoying the sense – or was it the sensation? – that she had passed out of her present time, and had begun, tentatively, to look around her and explore her own presence in whatever world she was in.

The scene changed before her eyes, and a deep forest sprang into being all around her, blurring into shape like the stones of the cottage in the cove. Yet the trees did not waver and die back into the air as had the cottage, but grew and aged all in a moment, becoming massive trunks hoary with moss and hanging vines and spreading darkness. The air became close and heavy, the density of the trees a brake against any wind that might blow through. Overhead rooks circled and called to each other. The air wavered as it does when heat rises on a hot day. She smelled smoke, and, looking up, saw a great billow laced with flame mounting into a sullen sky. Something big was burning. She could hear the crackle and rush of fire, could see through the smoke and flames the gaunt tall shape of a blackened chimney standing out against the air. She felt an overwhelming sensation of loss, of a bereavement too enormous to be borne.

Still in the grief, she became aware of some heavy body crashing through the underbrush of the forest. Before she had time to be afraid, a huge, rounded shape like a boulder on short legs came charging across the space where she stood. It was a wild boar, shouldered and tusked and bristled like some prehistoric monster, like the boar god himself, with wicked little red eyes and breathing a feral smell of rage and age and bestiality that nearly overpowered her. The boar did not see her, but the momentum of its charge brought it so close that she could still feel the wind of its rush when the sound of its passing had died away again in the distance. Around her the trees rustled, talking to one another in a language she recognized but could not understand.

She had scarcely caught her breath from the episode when the world changed again. The trees were even bigger now, but there were fewer of them and there were distant open areas visible through the widely spaced trunks. The air was fresher and brighter, as if the sun were breathing through the forest. Mick was standing in a little clearing, and she called to him, but he did not hear her. He stooped and picked up something from the ground and put it in his pocket. Then a shape began to grow around him, first a sagging rooftree, then half-transparent walls and a banging door that swung in the wind, and then a ramshackle hut rippled into being, its shape wavering and unsteady, as when rising heat distorts the air. Within the hut, Mick was sitting at a table lighted by a stub of candle anchored in its own wax. As she watched, the candle grew like a miniature tree putting out leaves and branches until it became a towering, many-armed candelabra whose light played over a great banquet table with seven guests, and she was one of them. She saw herself smiling and *laughing and then that too faded, replaced by a momentary vision of the little attic room and herself in bed.*

For a split second she fancied she really was in bed and waking from a dream that she tried to gather and recall. But the fragments defeated her memory, and she realized that her exhausted eyes and mind were playing tricks. She was standing in the little bedroom, fingers clutched so tight to the window-sill that they were white. How long she stayed there she had no idea. When some time later she crept back to bed, ice-cold and shivering uncontrollably, she was shocked to see Mick's head on the pillow, tranquil, innocent, deep in sleep. The peaceful rumble of his snore was the only sound in the room. That, and her own harsh breathing. She felt her mind spinning out of control, and held to the bedpost to keep from falling. It only lasted a moment. Then she slid carefully between the covers so as not to wake Mick, pulled the sheet up as far as it would go, and lay staring wide-eyed. Now, when she desperately wanted the solace and oblivion of sleep, it would not come. She watched the grey window at her bedside flower into primrose with the early light.

Party Time

Mick was surprised at how little trouble he had persuading Kath to stay in bed and rest next day. With uncharacteristic meekness she acceded to all his suggestions, ate when she was told to — though very little — and napped off and on for the better part of the day. When he inquired how she had slept, she insisted that she had slept the night through, wakened by no night noises, troubled by no uneasy dreams. Mick left her to rest. He spent much of his time in the kitchen with Greenie, who kept his coffee cup filled and answered his questions in between trips to the stove, the pantry, and the shed at the back, where a pig's carcass, having been hung upside down overnight, was now being readied for roasting. This, she explained, was to be the main dish and centerpiece of the feast.

"Tiernon was telling me a bit about it at dinner," said Mick. "But from what he said, I gather the food's the least part of the celebration."

"I wouldn't say that. Food's a big part of the goings-on. Only everything's all of a piece, the food and the ritual; they go together, don't you see."

"I suppose eating's a kind of ritual in itself."

"It is when I do the cooking," said Greenie.

"But surely," Mick persisted, "not every little snack or sandwich has the same weight as a full meal."

Greenie looked at him sideways. "You can't be as stupid as all that, a bright young fellow like you. You must know better. Did you never say grace? Never give thanks for the food you were about to eat?"

"Oh sure. And of course that's a ritual, I'm just so used to it . . ."

"But you think us country folk are bound to have different rituals—weird, primitive ones—way out here in the wilderness."

Caught with my notebook showing, thought Mick, and he grinned ruefully. "No, no, of course not. I'm sorry if I sounded . . . patronizing. You said it right—I'm ignorant. It's just that what Tiernon was telling me about sounded more formal, more ceremonial. It had to do with the whole year; plus, it was all tied up with nature, not just. . . ." He tailed off in growing embarrassment. "Yeah, I guess you're right."

Again she looked at him, not sideways this time, but full in the face. "Well. You've the grace to admit it, anyhow; that's something. You'll do, Mick, when you decide to stop asking and start listening. You might even learn something. Here, hold this, will you?" She handed him a vast bowl filled with a rich, golden egg batter and flavored with some spice or herb he could not identify, but which scented the whole kitchen with its fragrance.

"What's this?"

"It's the Solstice Cake for after the dinner, or will be when it's baked."

"Smells wonderful. What's in it?"

"Oh, different things. Eggs of course, but all new-laid, all brought in today from the farms. And honey beaten in. And flour. And crushed wheat and barley to give it body. And then just any old thing you have in the kitchen: currants and bits of apple and candied fruit. Pears and cherries and suchlike. It's an old recipe. You can beat the batter if you like. For luck. Here's a spoon."

He was handed a spoon the size of a canoe paddle and told to stir vigorously and make sure there were no flour lumps.

"For if there are lumps, the cake won't rise, and that would spoil the party."

Mick applied himself to the task, beating until the batter was smooth as cream, not a flour lump in sight, though the bits of fruit gave it some character.

"Now, if you don't mind, just tip it into this pan, and we'll pop it in the oven."

Pan, my foot, thought Mick. *That's a bathtub*. But he obligingly poured. The bathtub was popped into the oven and in a very short time a fragrance redolent of all the world's spices filled the kitchen.

"Is that the cake I'm smelling? What gives it that wonderful smell?"

"Just odds and ends. But they mix all together, and that makes it come out special. My old mum used to say that smell could wake the dead and revive the dying."

It was enough to revive Kath, as he found when he was released from kitchen duty late in the afternoon to see how she was doing. She was up and dressed, and met him at the top of the stairs. Their greetings overlapped.

"I was just coming down to find you."

"I was coming upstairs to find you."

"What's that delicious smell? Like cinnamon and clove and nutmeg and allspice and chocolate and orange and raspberries and everything all mixed together."

"Ah, that's a secret. Greenie's cake batter. She said it was enough to revive the dying and wake the dead. Looks like it woke the sleeping beauty."

"Well, something woke me, I'm not sure what. But I did sleep like the dead, so it might have been the cake. I'm all ready for this party of yours."

He was aware that she was electric with some suppressed emotion sparking just beneath the surface.

"The party hasn't started yet, Sleeping Beauty. I was going to rouse you with a kiss. We could . . . go on from there, if you're in the right mood. That is, if you'd like to be . . . aroused by a kiss."

She responded almost too eagerly.

"Why Mick, you romantic old thing, what a perfect fairy tale proposition. I'd love to be aroused by a kiss, and there's nobody I'd rather have do the kissing. Or the arousing. That is," she inquired, "if we have time?"

"Kath, my beautiful sleeper, we have all the time we need."

He took her arm, turned her around, and together they walked back down the hall to the bedroom, opened the door, went in and shut it after them.

Roast Boar

When at last they emerged, hand in hand like children, their faces were smoothed and shining, and their eyes were bright and slightly blurry, carrying even now their memory of a closeness too intimate for any sense but touch. Kath moved with luxurious lassitude, and Mick was aware that the latent emotional electricity, while still there, was noticeably diminished. Perhaps their lovemaking had drawn off some of the current.

When they got downstairs, Kath was surprised to find the inn deserted. They walked out the front door, and found the only sign of life to be a little girl energetically jumping rope near the old well and the tree-stump it guarded.

She seemed isolated in the private world that the very young sometimes inhabit, alone with her imagination, chanting a rhyme as she jumped:

> "I know a secret I won't tell.
> Promise that you'll keep it
> like a snail inside a shell.
> Cause if you say it out loud,
> it turns into a spell
> and makes a special magic.
> that's hidden in the well."

She did not look up as they passed.

"Where's the party, Mick?" said Kath. "You promised me a party."

When they walked into the clearing behind the Inn, the party was in full swing: a combination cookout and barn dance as nearly as Kath could tell. People were standing about, chatting, sipping beer or wine or the potent local cider, nibbling snacks. Small children ran in and out, whooping and shouting and chasing one another. For so remote a backwater community, there were a surprising number of people in attendance. Some were typical summer people, tourists staying at The Wicken Tree and looking for a little local color, but quite a few seemed native inhabitants come out of the Wickens both Great and Little, or out of the woodwork. *Or maybe just out of the wood*, Kath said to herself. The evening was clear and calm, the air so still that no leaf trembled. Kath looked about her. The scene reminded her of the odd, artificial look of the tree trunks in the headlights where Mick had first stopped the car. *An eternity ago.*

A ring of oaks, tall and spreading, enclosed a circle of smooth, short turf. Within this second circle was a third, a huge central firepit from which smoke rose straight to the sky. Close to the bonfire, the heat was almost too much, for the evening air was mild. In the heart of the fire, the logs had burned down to a bed of bright coals that seemed to pulse and shimmer with their own inner life. The edges of the pit were a fence of rippling flames turned transparent by the colorless light. *They look like water*, thought Kath, *reflected off a ceiling, like light reflected off water. Flames that are waves.* She did not speak aloud, but the words seemed to ring through the clearing, echoing off her unspoken thought like a delayed echo coming back from a distance. Startled, she looked to see if everyone else had heard them, but it seemed that no one had.

Above the fire an enormous hog, its forelegs and hindquarters stretched out and securely lashed fore and aft, was revolving on an iron spit. From a distance it looked like it was swimming in the air. The head with its tusks was still intact, the open jaws seeming to devour the spit that impaled it. The angry, red little eyes, fixed in death but still open, glared furiously through the heat, and Kath felt their gaze fall directly on her with every turn. As the carcass slowly revolved, savory juices trickled down the crisping sides to fall hissing and sizzling on the coals, and the good smell of slow-roasting meat mingled with the pungent tang of smoke from the fire. Over on one side but keeping a careful eye on the process, stood Tiernon, the man in the green jacket.

Master of the Revels? she wondered. He radiated authority as the pig radiated heat, and she remembered the jolt of eye-contact that had bothered her. The sight of the impaled carcass nagged at her memory. She tried, but could not get hold of why it was bothersome. Yet it haunted her. *This is a dream*, she thought.

Her thought fled from its own remembrance, but the fleeing took some effort, and she had to tell herself firmly that no, she did not have a headache. Reluctant to look at what was clearly the centerpiece of the celebration, she retreated mentally and physically, backing away from the fire and its revolving occupant to find a place just inside the circle of oak trees where she could watch without participating. *Roast Boar*, she told herself, in quotes. *How medieval. We should all be in costume.* Even without costumes, there was a certain theatricality in the scene, a sense of performance. *It's the bonfire, she decided. It's a throwback to the primitive. We're all primitives at heart, and an outdoor fire just brings it out. We could all be dancing around the flames and pouring libations to the gods.* She noticed that a couple of the older children were doing just that: dancing around the fire like the goblins at a party and pouring their soft drinks on the flames to hear the hiss and see the steam. She saw Mick chatting easily to a group of people a little distance away. And Tiernon was watching Mick. Feeling a little shy, she went up to him.

"Uhm . . . I want to thank you for . . . for helping me the other day. Mick told me . . . "

He brushed it aside with a gesture. "No thanks called for. You were our guest. I'm glad to see you better. That's a beauty of a bruise you've got, there around your right eye. Take a couple of days to fade, that will. I hope you can enjoy the party."

"I'm fine, really. I'm not actually the fainting type, you know. I was more just tired than anything."

"You know best," he said, not believing it.

Here came the same odd shift of balance she had felt at their meeting on the path. To ease the tension, she said the first thing that came into her head.

"What comes next? Is there some sort of ceremony?" It came out hopelessly inane and stupid, and even to her own ears the words sounded like empty babble.

Worse yet, at just that moment a snatch of conversation from the people talking with Mick came drifting their way: ". . . friends who always celebrate the Solstice . . . make a big ceremony of it in their back garden . . . It's a real ritual, they wrote it themselves, they have drums and a pan-pipe so there's music and dancing and . . . we went last year, dressed up as druids . . . Our little girl is with us this year . . . she loves all that kind of stuff."

The look on Tiernon's face told Kath all she needed to know.

"They're not as foolish and frivolous as they sound, you know," she told Tiernon. She tried to explain. "It's more than just a fad. They're looking for something." She remembered her earlier, playful conversation with Mick that first night, a time that now seemed like years ago instead of days. *Everybody's looking for something. Sweet dreams are made of this.*

What are you looking for? Tiernon had not spoken, but he was looking at her intently as the words reverberated in her mind.

"Who am I to disagree?" It was a relief to find Mick at her elbow, glass in hand. "Enjoying the party, Kath?" And to Tiernon, "She's a different woman from the one we carried up the path a couple of days ago, isn't she? A few more days, and she'll be her old self."

Relief at Mick's distraction changed to sudden, unreasoning irritation. Why must he be everlastingly harping on the state of her health? She was feeling just fine, thank you, and didn't need to be reminded otherwise.

"Oh, really? And just what is that old self, I'd like to know? Seems like you know me better than I do."

He ducked and threw up his hands in mock terror, but she was well started and she went on.

"I am my old self. I'm not tired and I'm not sick and I'm not dreaming and I'm not hallucinating and I only have one self and this is it. I know who I am and I know where I am and I wish you'd just . . ."

Heads were turning and Mick and Tiernon stared at her open-mouthed.

She dropped her voice and continued more quietly, " . . . just quit nagging."

Mick shook his head as from an actual blow. "Okay, lady, anything you say. Everything's fine and dandy. Just don't kill me, all right? Hey, I'm the guy you came with, remember?"

Tiernon was watching her curiously. She remembered what he had said about strangers. *It's us that have to look you over and find out who you are.*

"I'm sorry, Mick." She stood on tiptoe and kissed him on the cheek. "Lost my cool for a minute."

161

Mick slipped his arm around her and returned the kiss. Turning to Tiernon, he steered the conversation into a smoother channel. "You folks certainly celebrate the Solstice in style. When does the ceremony get underway?"

"Not long now," said Tiernon, "but you mustn't expect anything . . . elaborate. We're simple folks around here. Nothing fancy." His words answered Mick, but his look was for Kath. He continued. "We have to wait for the moon to rise."

One of the bedsheet people jumped into the conversation, giving Mick some unexpected help. "I've never seen a pig that large. He looks like a cave painting." He turned to his daughter standing near, and Mick recognized the girl with the jump-rope. "Look there honey. Doesn't he look like the one we saw in the caves last year? You remember, the one on the wall that looked like it moved in the torchlight?"

She nodded, and moved closer to her father and safety.

"Ah, he's no painting, this boyo," said Tiernon. "There are still a few tuskers like him running wild through the woods. You have to know where to find them, where they hide out."

"How long will he take to be done?"

"A big lad like this one here? He'll take a good long time to cook through. He's been over the fire for most of the day. He ought to be proper done pretty soon now."

At that moment a pearlescent glow behind the trees announced the moon's rising. In scant minutes its disc appeared, steadily mounting, steadily growing until the whole brilliant round was in view. So big that it seemed within reach, it cast a shimmer of silver over the earth and everything in it. The effect was magical. Voices hushed, faces turned skyward toward the enchantment. The spell lasted for maybe a minute, and then, with moonrise as the signal, people began to gather around the fire, ready for the feast.

Tiernon unhooked the spit from its mooring, swung it clear of the coals, and brought it to rest over a vast wooden trough set to catch the drippings. With a strange, mute dignity that transcended his death and approaching dismemberment, the pig glared defiance at the humans preparing to eat him. Two burly men stepped out of the crowd and, one on either side, they grasped the head, and

Kath saw with no surprise that it was separate from the body.

The boar had been decapitated and his component parts re-assembled on the spit for roasting. She thought herself away from the memory of the gash across the throat, the pouring blood and forced herself to be a disinterested spectator. It almost worked. Carefully, the two men slid the head free of its iron spike and set it on an immense platter that Tiernon held ready. The platter was then placed ceremoniously on an elevated stone platform positioned opposite the fire. It faced out toward the assembly.

The crowd of people fell silent. Tiernon turned and faced them. He seemed taller and older. When he spoke his voice reverberated through the clearing like the sounding of a horn. "Friends, guests, all who've been called to celebrate this Solstice and help the sun return, we welcome you. We ask your help in sending our prayer to the world that is the other side of our own. Join in our sacrifice and our feast."

From the circle of people he took the arm of a woman and led her forward. She came with deliberate pace, but slowly and haltingly, and Kath saw that it was Lame Elly. She hadn't seen her up to now, and wondered where she could have been. *It's not that big a crowd*, she thought. *I surely would have noticed if she'd been here.*

Mick was more vocal. "Well, I'll be darned. How'd she get here? I thought she could hardly walk. Look, Kath that's . . ."

"Hush that!" she said without thinking. And then more softly, "Quiet, Mick. She's going to speak."

She was indeed. The crowd had fallen silent, and into the silence Lame Elly's voice fell like water into a still pond. The language was unintelligible, no tongue that Kath or Mick had ever heard.

"I thought as much. She's talking to the pig." Thus Mick in an aside to Kath. "It's some sort of invocation. This is even better than I expected."

Kath turned to Greenie, standing near them.

"What language is that? What's she saying?"

"She's using the old language. He won't understand any other. The Invocation comes first." She translated:

"Messenger.
Speak for us
when you go
from the feast
made of you
made for you
made by your favor.
Be our prayer
as you go.
Send back the Sun.
Heal the Tree.
Fill the Well.
See they join
for your return."

Now Elly tilted the cup she carried, and poured a liquid stream directly on the pig's head. The cider ran down the nose and cheeks, and trickled into the open mouth. Kath could have sworn that the pig's mouth widened to receive the libation, and the head appeared almost imperceptibly to nod. It was a trick of the firelight, of course, the play of light and shadow that made things appear to move. Again, Elly spoke in the old language, and again Greenie translated, but it seemed to Mick that she was explaining more for Kath's benefit than for his.

"She's asking him to speak to the sun for us, to say farewell and ask the sun not to forget us, not to forget that we need him to come back in his season, we need the sun to bring the light and the warm."

Elly turned and her blind gaze encompassed the circle of silent, watching people. And now she spoke so all could understand.

"He accepts our asking," she announced. "He'll carry our message. We can be sure, he speaks for us. The Sun will come back. And we can hope that the Well will fill and water the Tree, the Tree will heal, and the Door be open." She turned back to the head on its platform, speaking again in the ancient tongue.

"She's thanking him, now,'" said Greenie. "Telling him the feast is in his honor and inviting him to join."

Leaving Kath and Mick, Greenie stepped forward, and Kath saw that she had a large carving knife in her hand. The knife seemed viciously sharp, a weapon rather than a utensil. Involuntarily Kath closed her eyes against the sight, fighting to shut out the memory it wakened.

Greenie made a ceremonial first slice into the loin, bisected it with a second, and removed the outside cut. Tiernon held out an empty plate. Deftly Greenie slid the meat onto the plate, and Tiernon laid it ceremoniously in front of the boar's head, saying something again in the incomprehensible tongue.

No. No. No! Kath heard her own voice cry out in silent protest, but no one seemed to hear. The boar would devour himself and they, the celebrants, would join in the feast. They also would eat him. She knew it. She had expected it.

"What do you suppose he's saying now?" whispered Mick, and Kath turned in surprise.

"He just invited the boar to eat. Didn't you hear?"

"Don't tell me you understood what he was saying?"

Kath started to answer, but was cut off by Greenie, who called out, "Who's hungry? Who'll be next?"

Kath wanted to turn and run, but she could not move. She was being assaulted by images that came too fast to resist: the terrible rush of the huge boar in the forest, men bringing the killed boar home from the hunt, the blood pouring out the deep gash in the throat. She looked up to see that the grizzled men were watching her.

Greenie was cutting a second slice now, and sliding it onto the plate Tiernon held out. Carefully, wielding the terrible knife, she cut a bite-sized chunk off the slice. Tiernon offered the plate to Kath.

"Guest next," he told her.

She took an instinctive step back, but Tiernon's steady gaze gave her no way of escape. His face was serious to the point of sternness, his hand holding out the plate was firm, and his eyes commanded her.

"Take it, Kath, for heaven's sake," Mick muttered. "You're being bloody rude."

Her hands were shaking, but she reluctantly accepted the plate, and felt Mick relax beside her. Tiernon gave a slight nod of approval and encouragement.

Greenie chimed in. "Now you eat up. This will do you good. Put some strength into you."

The smell of the roasted meat invaded her nostrils. She thought irrationally of Lamb's *Dissertation upon Roast Pig*, but it didn't help.

Her stomach turned over. *How will I eat this?* Kath asked herself. *I cannot do it.*

Mick saw her hesitation, but misread it utterly. "Come on, listen to Greenie now, Kath. You're still way behind on your meals and you've got to get your appetite back."

Kath looked in rising panic at Greenie and realized that Greenie was looking at her with the same watchfulness that she had seen in Tiernon. She was watching to see what Kath would do, waiting to judge her. So was Tiernon. The silence grew, becoming a large bubble that enclosed Kath and isolated her from the rest of the world. With sudden self-consciousness Kath realized that it was not just Tiernon and Greenie; everyone was watching her.

This is a test, thought Kath, and then, *this is crazy. I will not do this. I will not be in this ceremony, whatever it is. I don't want it. I will not be a part of it.* She would not let herself know she was afraid.

You are a part of it whether you will or no, said Tiernon's eyes.

A soft voice broke her bubble, interrupting the unspoken dialogue.

"It's a very old custom in these parts, my dear. It's a formality. You have only to take one bite, the ritual first bite, and then everyone else can begin to eat, and they'll stop staring at you." It was Elly, her blind gaze reading Kath with perfect understanding.

I cannot do this, Kath protested silently. *Don't make me do it.*

You can do it. Elly's thought answered her thought.

Kath said aloud, "I don't have a fork."

"Use your fingers," said Greenie.

"Kath for heaven's sake!" said Mick.

There was no way out. Kath picked up the bite-sized piece, held it for a moment, then slowly put it in her mouth and chewed doggedly. It tasted gamey, old and savage in the back of her mouth, and she gagged but managed to turn the gag into a swallow. Forcing the morsel down her throat took considerable effort, but she got it done, then looked about her. Mick was looking relieved, Greenie had already turned back to the pig and was cutting more slices and putting them onto the plates the eager crowd held out to her. Tiernon simply nodded his head.

It was blind Elly, who could not possibly have seen what Kath did, who said softly,

"There now. That was well done and it's over. You've nothing more to fear."

But Kath had taken the beast into her body, and she was afraid.

The Crack in the Teacup

The rest of the party passed in a dream. Kath stuck close to Mick, drank more cider, chatted animatedly to this person and that, heard herself saying "Yes, indeed, a lovely party, certainly is a beautiful evening, no we didn't know, we're just lucky to have stopped here right at this time." The denuded carcass of the boar, a mute sacrifice to appetite and fresh air, lolled grotesquely from the spit. The head presided, glaring fiercely on the festivities.

A voice spoke at her elbow. "You're not eating anything."

She looked at Tiernon, aware that he knew, aware that he knew her knowledge as well.

"I'm not hungry," she told him. "I had the one bite and that was enough. You made me take that, but I can't eat any more of . . . I just can't eat any more. You know why."

"Is it the eating that's worrying you? I thought it was the killing."

"The whole thing is worrying me. I don't know what to say or think, or how to feel. Ever since I came here . . . "

"What since you came here? "

"I don't know. I'm all confused."

"If it's the pig . . . "

"What if it is? The pig is just a part of it. Because it's more than a pig."

He didn't deny it. "Well, now, you mustn't mind about that. It isn't the shape we honor, but what's inside the shape. It's the energy that's holy."

Before she could respond she heard a shout. It took two to carry the tray with the cake, a vast round, brown and crusty and redolent of spices.

"Time for the cake," called Greenie.

The cake, which had apparently been baking almost as long as the pig had been roasting, matched it in size. It took two men to carry it out and deposit it on a table. Greenie was cutting into it, and Tiernon was handing round slices to the crowd that gathered to eat it. The smell was spicy and sweet, but heady with memories she didn't dare let in. She couldn't eat it, though she could taste the batter on her tongue. Her stomach heaved. She shook her head mutely when Tiernon offered her a slice.

"Still not eating anything? Would you like some more cider?"

"I've had enough." She laughed shakily. "I'm already feeling a bit swimmy. I'd better go easy."

"Look at the bottom of the cup," said Tiernon, holding it out to her.

She looked down, expecting—what? Tea leaves? A fortune-telling? She didn't know. But there was nothing in the bottom of the cup. It was quite empty. Still she stared. It was the same cup, the one she seemed always to be given, the one with the missing handle, chipped edge, and the long crack down the side and clear across the bottom. Stained black from years of use, the crack was so deeply incised she was prepared for the cup to fall apart, yet it remained intact. Cracked, but whole.

"Keep looking," he said.

She couldn't not look. The crack in the cup drew her eyes like a magnet, pulling her down and into itself. As she gazed the crack opened, widening immeasurably, obliterating the cup itself, blocking out her hand holding it, engulfing the world in which she stood. She saw it coil in on itself, curving and re-curving in the familiar pattern that yet was a puzzle with the mystery at the heart of it. She was afraid of falling. She was afraid of wanting to fall. She felt herself falling.

Seeing her sway, Mick started forward. The light touch of Greenie's hand on his arm immobilized him.

"Let be," said Greenie.

He tried to shake off her arm and found himself powerless. He could not move.

"Let go of me, will you? She's in trouble, she needs help."

"She'll take no harm. Tiernon will go with her," said Greenie.

"Go with her where? She shouldn't be going anywhere. She's ill, can't you see? *Will* you let go?"

"It's you that has to let go, not me. Let her go." Greenie released his arm.

He turned on her in fear and anger. "What in hell do you people think you're doing? If anything happens to her . . . "

It was not Greenie who answered him but Lame Elly, her sightless eyes soft with sympathy.

"Nothing will happen to her but what should happen. Be easy in your mind. She is stronger than you think, your Kath. She will come through it. If you truly want to help her. "

"Of course I want to help her." His voice was out of control, he was shouting now, and people were turning to stare. "I love her. And you people—"

"Are her people." Greenie finished his sentence. "If you love her, Mick, then let your love go with her."

He watched, unable to move, helpless to stop what happened. He saw Kath turn to look at Tiernon, but so slowly that she might have been asleep, or under water. He saw him stretch out his hand to her and saw her reach her hand into his. Darkness surged over them, whelming them like an incoming tide.

The Shadow and the Beast

It seemed to Kath that they went a long way into darkness. Out of time and out of space they walked. At first she could feel nothing but Tiernon's hand that gripped her own. At first she could see nothing but the darkness of a dream where the dreamer is the only presence. At first she could hear no sound, but presently she heard from a great distance the sound of a bird's cry, three plaintive descending notes, over and over. The sound reverberated against rocky walls and blended with the ceaseless boom and echo of waves as they dashed against the cliffs. Then she saw the bird. It was just in front of them, fluttering down the path.

She stopped. Motionless on the steep path. The wind was blowing strongly. All around them the *waves boomed and crashed, and the walls thrummed and echoed with the sound.*

"Where are we going?"

Tiernon swung her around to face him and dropped her hand.

He said, "To the center."

His voice was harder than she remembered. The edge of it cut through the booming sound of the waves like a knife and stopped her breath. He said, "You must go in."

Her eyes widened in sudden terror. She said, "No. I don't want this. It's the bridge. I don't want to cross this bridge."

She was shaking from head to foot. He put his hands on her shoulders and she thrummed under his touch like rock walls when the sea beats at them. The sound swelled until it filled the air, drowning out the boom of the waves.

He said, "You must cross. It's the pattern. It must be. It has always been. You can't not want it."

She said, "I am afraid of wanting it."

He said, "Use the fear."

She said, "How do I use fear?"

He said, "By going to meet it, by following where it leads." He turned her to face it.

Before her was the rock face and the spiral at eye level, filling all space. She shook her head, like one trying to wake from sleep. "I can't go into a wall."

"You haven't tried. Go on."

"How?"

"One step at a time."

She stared at the spiral, a flat pattern of line against a flat stone surface. She stepped forward and found herself within the maze.

Then there was only silence, rippling like flames in sunlight, like sunlight reflected off water, like light on water reflected up on a ceiling. The booming of the waves was a distant echo on the outer edge of hearing. Everything fell away behind her. Tiernon was gone. Everything before this moment was gone. The maze, no flat pattern now but a curving tunnel, unwound ahead of her one step at a time, the rock walls bending around and closing in on her. In terror she moved forward, giving herself to the labyrinth. The curve and re-curve, the double-back and turn-again of the pattern was a rhythm that imprisoned her, swinging her forward and flinging her back, twisting and turning until all direction was lost. She was blind, with only the next turn to guide her, and the next and the next. The walls hemmed her in, and she could see neither ahead nor behind. There was no future and no past, only an endless now that *went on and on. She came to a crossing and stopped bewildered. One way held a shadow, a man-shape leaning on a club made of shadows, waiting for her. The other held a mystery, something ancient and savage at the heart of the maze. She felt her heart slow down, each heartbeat echoing in eternity. She said, "I can't choose. I don't want to choose. I am not ready for this." She cried out in panic. "Mick! Help me, Mick! I am lost. I need you."*

Bewildered, angry, hostile, Mick wanted to fight, to yell, to force an answer out of somebody. "What have you done to her?"

"Nothing," answered Elly. "We've done nothing to her. No one has harmed her."

"Be easy, Mick," said Greenie.

"Easy be damned!" he shouted. "She's in trouble. You've done something to her. You've given her some damned thing to make her sleep."

He was like a stag brought to bay, facing the hunters. He couldn't read their faces as they stared back at him. Or rather, he couldn't trust or even believe what he read. The faces were surprised, concerned, even kindly, but they all shut him out of what was happening. They made a circle, and he was outside it. He looked around him at the rest of the party. The other guests, plates in hand, seemed to be in a different world altogether. They were laughing, chatting, clearly unaware of the drama going on in their midst. Mick felt the panicked isolation of a man in a nightmare, trapped in a cone of silence, forced to see but helpless to act.

Kath was like a woman under water, her blind and open eyes fixed on some unseen distance. She didn't look at him when he reached out to her; she made no response when Greenie took her arm and led her like a sleepwalker to a place under the trees. Like a sleepwalker returning to her bed, she lay down on the grass. Greenie covered her with a shawl.

Then she turned to him. "Mick, I swear to you by sunlight and starlight, we have done nothing to her. We don't control what happens. She does. Now we must wait for her to come back. And she will come back."

"Wait! For how long? Come back from where? Where is she?"

"She is in the other place. Time passes differently there, so we cannot interfere. We cannot touch her, where she is. You cannot touch her. Only he can touch her, and she him.

It must happen, every year. To try to bring her back would . . . would do great damage."

"Damage? To Kath?"

"To everything."

He felt Tiernon's hands on him, restraining him, and, like an exhaled breath, the fight went out of him. His shoulders sagged, and he stepped back, shaking his head like a bewildered bear, shrugging off the hands. He looked at Kath, lying so still under the tree. Her blind eyes were wide open. They stared unseeing, and he knew that she was lost to him and he to her.

"Only for this present moment," said Greenie. "If you bring her back now, it will all be lost, all for nothing. And she will not forgive you. You must let be."

Kath lay motionless on the grass, her breathing even, but so shallow he could scarcely see the rise and fall. "I won't touch her," he said. "But she will come back? You say she will come back?"

"I say it," said Greenie. "It is only this night. When the sun turns, she will come back. It will have happened, the mating. She will bring him back. She will bring the sun back."

"But what is happening? What is this other place?"

"You thought it was just stories, didn't you?" asked Elly, and her blind eyes pierced him. "You thought they were just something we made up for amusement on a long evening? You were going to write them down and put them in a book and sell it on the bookstalls and make a lot of money?"

Mick started to protest but Elly kept right on talking.

"I tell you they are not just stories, and they are not yours to sell. They are our birthright, they are what we live by, they are who we are. They are not yours, and you cannot take them so. You collect the bits and pieces, and you call them stories, but you don't know that they're all parts of the same story, a very long story that's been going on forever. And it's still going on. And we are in it. All of us. All the time."

Mick brushed a hand over his eyes like a man who has stumbled into a cobweb where the path seemed clear. No one moved, no one looked at him.

"You come here," she said, "looking for what you don't know. I tell you that you will find it, and you will not know it when you see it."

He felt time slow down, each moment an eternity.

Kath stirred, turned, restless and uneasy in the enchanted sleep.

She said, "I can't choose. I don't want to choose. I am not ready for this." She cried out in panic. "Mick! Help me, Mick! I am lost. I need you."

Her voice was silent, but he heard her.

Elly cried out, "Something's slipped! She's changing the story. Wake her up!"

Greenie looked at Tiernon, but he was kneeling by Kath, one arm under her shoulder.

Mick took her away from him, took her in his arms, "Don't touch her! She's not yours. You people are crazy. This whole thing is crazy."

Her lips moved and he bent to hear. She said, "Mick." She said, "The hell with this."

He told her, "Kath, I'm here. I'm holding you. It's all right."

Even as he spoke, Mick felt the story tugging at him, gathering strength and pulling him into itself as Tiernon looked at him. *I won't let it happen*, he thought.

"It's too late," said Tiernon. "She's moved into the story now."

"She hasn't moved anywhere," said Mick, "I've got her."

"No," Tiernon told him sadly. "No you don't."

"That's all you know. I'm keeping her."

"She isn't yours to keep. She belongs to the story and now so do you. Now we have to fight for her."

"I'll fight all right. I'm no part of your crazy story, but you can bet I'll fight to keep her out of your hands, you and your whole crew of nut cases."

Even as he declared "I'll fight," he could feel the words turning in his mouth, gaining power, surrounding him, possessing him as he repeated them until they became a spell, a summons that called him out of time and place into a spinning darkness that set him down in a little grove of trees where he knew the maiden who was Kath was watching, her hands twisted in her apron.

He was in it now, and though he didn't want to know it, he knew he was captured by the story, imprisoned in its moves and subject to its outcome. He and the other chieftain circled one another. He balanced on the balls of his feet, looking for an opening, watching as Tiernon did the same, balancing his spear to throw.

Every year, he heard himself thinking. *Every year we do this for the first time. It's always the same. Always new. This time I will win her.*

Sunlight and Sanity

The first sharp spear of sun hitting his eyelids woke Mick with a jolt. He sat up and looked about him, unsure of who or where he was. He was stretched full length on the ground next to the firepit whose cold ashes held the dregs of last night's feast. No one was around. Everyone had dissolved like mist when the sun comes out. And the dream—which had been so real that he felt the swing of the sword in his hand and the bitter iron of Tiernon's spear as it pierced him— was poised at the edge of the same mist. Without acknowledging what he was doing, he pushed it deep into the back of his memory. Willing it away, willing it to never have been, he seated himself safely, resolutely back in the daylight world, and it was hard and sharp and outlined in light. Kath lay beside him on the ground.

She was lying peacefully, breathing easy. Her eyes were closed in ordinary sleep.

Gently, tentatively, he touched her arm. Her eyes opened and she looked at him and she saw him. He went weak with relief.

"Good morning, Sunshine. Had a good sleep?"

"Mick. You're here. You're all right."

"Of course I'm all right. It's you I'm worried about. But let's not talk now. Let's get you up and around. Time enough later to sort things out." He hoped he was right.

Then he was shepherding her up the stone path to the house, one hand under her elbow. She seemed all right, a bit shaky, and cold from lying so long on the ground, but otherwise well enough. But this was Kath, he reminded himself. You never could tell. He steered her into the deserted common room, got her seated, went out to the kitchen. No one was around. The coffee pot was on the stove. Cold. He set it over a burner, adjusted the flame to warm but not boil, waited while it heated, found two cups, and poured. The coffee was thick and strong and black as thunder. He found the sugar firkin, ladled generous spoonfuls, stirred, carried the cups back to the common room.

She hadn't moved.

"Drink up," he said. "Here's to sunlight and sanity."

She took a sip, made a face, put the cup down. Her hands were shaking.

He took her hands in his to hold them still. *Sanity*.

"What's happened, and where is everybody? What's been going on?"

"You passed out at the party. Worried me sick to see you lying there. I didn't know what was going on and no one would tell me." He was not about to tell her what he'd heard from Greenie and Elly. Not now, anyway. *Just the facts, ma'am.* "And then I passed out too. Next thing I knew, the sun was in my eyes and it was tomorrow. Nobody was around. All gone to bed, I expect. And that's where you should be, my girl."

"Bed's fine. I could use a nap. But I'm hungry. I need more than coffee. Must not have eaten much at the party."

Something that disagreed with you, he thought, that's what you ate. But he didn't say it. She was talking too fast, the words tumbling out. He recognized the symptoms of shock. Her hands were icy.

She pulled them away to brush hair out of her eyes, and, with the hair, the memories that crowded her inner vision. It didn't work. Mick hitched forward on his chair. He took her hands again, gripped them tight. "Kath let's get out of here. This place is creepy; it's unwholesome. The people up here aren't telling stories. They're trying to live in them. And now they're making you do the same. Things have gone wrong ever since we got to this place. Half the time I've felt like I couldn't reach you, like you were someplace else. But what happened last night beats everything."

She pulled her hands away, then not to hurt him, cradled her coffee cup. To buy time she tried to take a sip, but her hand shook and the coffee spilled and dribbled down her chin.

With impatient tenderness Mick reached his napkin and dabbed at her face.

The simple gesture unlocked the door, letting in everything. She felt the start of panic, and grabbed the napkin from him to wipe away the angry tears that brimmed her eyes and threatened to spill over.

Mick looked at her carefully. "What happened just now to make you cry? You were seeing something, remembering something. What was it? I could see it in your face. And your eyes."

"The napkin."

"What about it?"

"It was in the dream. But it was an apron, not a napkin."

"Look, I know dreams have their own logic, but can you give me a little help here?"

"You wiped the coffee away with your napkin. She . . . I did that."

"Somebody wiped coffee off your face?"

"Not coffee. Blood. Not my face. His. She, I wiped his face with her apron, where the blood ran down."

"You keep saying 'She. I.' Was she you? And is he me? Was I in your dream?" Something was knocking at the door of his mind, urgent to be admitted. He refused to hear it, concentrating on Kath.

"She was me. Whoever I was when I changed. And he was . . . " A fresh spate of tears interrupted.

Mick handed her the napkin. "Here. Blow your nose."

She honked vigorously, sniffed, breathed deep.

"All right now?"

She wasn't all right, but she tried to be.

He tried as well. "Let's start over. What do you mean you changed? Into someone else? I saw you fall into some kind of trance sleep, but you didn't change."

She shook her head. "You wouldn't see it."

"Maybe we should start from the beginning, or as near the beginning as you can remember. Last night at the party, we were standing, talking, and somebody handed you a cup of cider and something happened to you. What was it?"

"I was . . . in a different place, not the party, all that disappeared. I can't remember how I came to be there, but it didn't seem to matter; I was just there, the way you are in dreams. And Tiernon was there, and he told me to follow the path, to go into the maze. The path went winding down and down with trees and bushes on either side, but it wasn't a path, it was the maze. It was dark. Not night-dark, but the dark you get in dreams where all you can see is the thing you're looking straight at. The maze went on forever, one turning, then another, and I'd think each one was the final one, and as soon as I passed it I'd see another turn up ahead.

"And then — this is where it gets scary, or at least where I started getting scared — I got to the center, and something was there; I don't know exactly what, just sort of a shape: a man with a boar's head standing with a club or a sword or some sort of weapon. And I saw you, and I knew you were going to fight. I remember saying, 'I can't choose.' And then you did fight. You and the boar-man were seriously trying to kill each other — rolling around and bashing at each other. But the funny thing was, with all that action there was no noise. It was like watching a silent movie. And the movie kept rewinding, so that I'd see the same thing over and over, the same two figures dodging and slashing at one another. Over and over. Then it changed, and you were swinging a scythe, like mowing a field, only it was the pig-man you were mowing. And then you were mowed down yourself because the other one gored you. You fell on the scythe blade, and it stuck up through your middle like a question mark. But a little later you were back swinging the scythe and the boar-man was coming for you again. And then I said, 'The hell with this.' I dodged just in time, and the pig-man was coming straight at me to gore me. At least, his mouth was open, but there was no sound. I thought for sure I was going to get that tusk in my guts. But I didn't. It went clean through me without touching me, and the man followed it in and through me like I was air. When I turned, he was crashing into you standing behind me, and you were solid enough. But I wasn't. Then the two of you were struggling with each other. Then the pig-man broke the grip and gored you, and you fell. But as you fell you said my name. That's when everything changed. That's when my head came apart. One half knew I was dreaming, and the other half didn't. It wasn't a movie anymore, and I wasn't watching; I was in it. I knew why I was there—because you were fighting over me. And it wasn't silent, because when you fell you looked straight at me. You said, 'Next year,' and your eyes rolled back in your head and you died. The other man, the pig-man who was still alive, stood up, his breath like cloth tearing. He looked right at me. He said, 'You are mine.' I almost said 'In a pig's eye, buster!' Because I knew him. I knew you both. But I also knew that he was right. That he'd won me. Again. That he always does.

"Then it wasn't even a dream anymore. It was real, and it was bad, and I realized that I was standing in someone else's shoes. I mean really, not a metaphor. I looked down at my feet and they were wearing wooden clogs caked with mud, and above them was a skirt and apron and clutching hands with red knuckles and dirt under the nails. They were not my hands and I knew that, but I could feel the cloth rough under my fingers. I was there in the flesh, but it wasn't my flesh. I felt the drag of my clogs in the mud as they walked forward. I saw your open wound, I smelled your sweat, I felt one of my hands take the apron and start to dab at the blood. Then I let go the apron, and the landscape dissolved like river mist and was gone, both men were gone, and all the noise was silence."

"That's some dream," said Mick.

"Some dream," she agreed, thinking *please let him stop now*.

He didn't stop. He wasn't going to stop. He was going to make her go through it all again.

"So, this man who was me in your dream, he died. And whoever you were wiped the blood away."

"Yes I did."

"When you were in the dream, did you know you were her? Did you have her feelings?"

"Yes, I knew I was her. Yes, I had her feelings. I was both of us; I was double and I couldn't do anything about it. And the feelings were horrible. Because . . ." She stopped.

Careful not to jar her, he waited.

". . . I don't know who I was but I knew who the two men were. You were one. And Tiernon was the other. And I'd seen something like it before, in another dream, a waking dream. And you kept switching identities, the way things blur and change in dreams. So I don't know which one of you killed the other. Only that it happened. And I couldn't stop it."

"I know those dreams, where you're convinced you're awake and then you wake up and you're still in the dream, still asleep. It's a recognized phenomenon, a combination of alpha and beta waves. Has a lot to do with body chemistry. And God knows yours is out of whack."

Here we go again, she thought. *Why is it always me who's out of whack? I'm tired of this game, tired of being "it."*

"I know that feeling, when something in waking life triggers a memory. It's not surprising that you'd dream about me, and not very surprising that you'd dream about Tiernon. He's been in and out of our orbit ever since the gab. So that explains that."

No it doesn't, she thought. *It just puts a frame around it. But it's the wrong frame.*

They were both quiet then, occupied in their own thoughts. The whole thing sounded absurd, even to her, and she wanted to dismiss it, to make it not have happened, but as she stared down at her hands she saw the blood dried under her fingernails.

The Reckoning

They were aware of another presence.

Greenie in the kitchen doorway. Now she came into the common room, fresh as lettuce, full of daylight, devoid of mystery. "There you are. Dead to the world when I saw you last, and then disappeared into thin air. Bed not slept in, car still there, or I might have thought you'd taken a drive to watch the sun rise."

She flicked an invisible crumb off the table, picked up the coffeepot, set it down. "Coffee already? That's boiled down to tar, that batch. I'll make some fresh. You look ready for early breakfast."

So it was to be over, the previous evening banished and forgotten.

But not quite. She looked at them narrowly. "Everything all right? No harm done. But if you will sleep out of doors in a wood on Midsummer Eve you shouldn't be surprised if you have dreams. Like the man in the play, you know. Bottom? The mummers put it on last summer in the field back of the house. Laughed myself silly at all those goings-on, donkey's heads and suchlike."

"And now the play is over, is that it?" said Mick. "The actors go home and everything goes back to where it was? You expect us to go along? Pretend that nothing happened?"

"I would if I was you," said Greenie. "Least said, soonest mended."

"So there is something to mend? At least you grant that much."

"Not for me to grant or withhold. Things are what they are. It's different, isn't it, Mick, when a story turns out real, when the things that happen in it really happen. Then it's not a way to pass an evening with the simple country folk, then it's not a story you can put between covers and close the book."

Mick brushed his hand over his eyes and lashed back.

"If it turns out there's any harm to Kath, I'm holding you responsible. You can do a lot of harm. You and your whole outfit."

"Harm, is it? We did no harm. We knew it would happen, and we couldn't change it, but we didn't cause it, whatever you think."

"But harm was done. Something went wrong, didn't it? Whatever was supposed to happen didn't happen. I heard Tiernon say it was a different story. So it was a story."

"Sometimes stories tell themselves," said Greenie. "They're stronger than the people in them."

All the while Kath had sat unspeaking, listening, looking at her fingernails. Now she spoke, to Greenie, not to Mick.

"It's me, isn't it? I'm the flash point, the hot spot that turns into a volcano. The story explodes into our lives, and it starts telling itself. And I am a part of it. One story didn't happen, because I took a different turning. The other story did happen, because I followed its path. If I hadn't been there, the two men wouldn't have fought. They wouldn't have had to fight."

201

"But the fight wasn't real," declared Mick. "Nobody was killed."

Not yet, thought Kath. But he could not hear her thought, and she did not speak it.

He went on. "I've read all about the Solstice and bringing back the sun and all those agricultural myths about fertility. But whether or not a meeting took place, whether or not a . . . a mating took place" — he glanced at Kath and glanced away again — "the sun came up this morning as it always does, ritual or no ritual, ceremony or no ceremony."

"Ritual or no ritual!" The scorn in Greenie's voice was palpable. "What you think rituals are for? For the fun of it? For the sun? They're for us, to put ourselves right with the world, to stay in the rhythm."

"Rhythm be damned," said Mick. "Even if Elly was right, even if Kath got into the wrong story, that didn't change anything. It didn't alter the way the world works."

Greenie was indignant. "You city people, you want everything to happen all at once, like in the films. How would you know anything about the way the real world works, always looking at a book and never at the sky?"

He started to protest, but she steamrollered over him.

"How can you tell what's changed without you pay attention, without you watch the year turn itself? See if the corn comes up full in the ear, if there's fish in the sea and beasts in the wood. There was no mating last night. Well, that will change things. But it will happen so slow you'll not notice it until the sky is different, until you haven't enough to eat." She stopped, took a breath, and visibly shifted gears. "Waste of time, telling folks what they don't know how to hear. Breakfast in half a tick." She snatched up the coffeepot and vanished through the swing door.

"Wow," said Mick. "She's as angry as I am. But Kath, more than Greenie or me, I'm concerned about you. Something is happening to you, whether it's happening to the rest of the world or not. Let's get out of here. Go back to civilization. And don't you dare say 'whatever that is.' It's sanity and daylight and dreams that stay put and don't come roaring into real life and play merry hell with who we are."

"But Mick, what about Elly and her stories? What about your great find and all your hopes? That's why we came here, isn't it? You can't give it all up because of me. I just went through a bad patch, that's all, and you got stuck in it. Why don't I clear out and go back to civilization and leave you here to keep working?"

"Because I'm sick of this place and everything in it. Lame Elly and Mr. Smarty-pants Tiernon and Greenie and all her talk. And as for the project, I'm sick of that too. No more airy fairy nonsense. I'll get a different job, digging ditches, or selling toothpaste. Something sane and sensible that will benefit humanity."

She managed a smile. He was working so hard. But so was she. It took effort to not look at her fingernails.

"Don't be silly, Mick. This is your career we're taking about. I won't let you chuck it just because of a bad weekend. Besides, you'd be a terrible toothpaste salesman. And you're a good folklorist."

"Alright, so that was a figure of speech. I'm not about to chuck years of work. What I meant was that right now I just want to get out, get away. And I want to get you away. Can't we at least try?"

"All right, Mick. We can try."

They were silent as Greenie came bustling back, her tray loaded with plates and silverware and napkins. She laid their places and disappeared again, reappearing in almost too short a time, the tray re-laden with a server piled with scrambled eggs, two racks of toast, a pot of jam, and a large square of butter. And a fresh pot of coffee that she plonked on the table like a punctuation mark. Period. Full stop.

"Eat up," she said, and disappeared back into her kitchen.

Civilization

They cleared out as soon as they finished breakfast, by which time the place was quiet except for themselves, the bedsheet druids sleeping it off, Greenie in retreat to the kitchen, Tiernon nowhere to be seen. No one appeared when they humped their luggage down the stairs and stowed it in the car. Mick left money for the bill on the hall dresser, feeling obscurely that with this he put paid to the whole affair. A final reckoning. Finished.

They pulled out of the car park and turned onto the road. "Civilization, here we come!" sang Mick, one-handed behind the wheel. Kath didn't sing, but she waved farewell.

She had washed her hands, and her fingernails were conspicuously clean.

As it always does, the way back seemed shorter.

Because we know where we're going, thought Mick.

Because we're going back, not forward, thought Kath.

They passed the place where she had seen the little dog. The road was empty. No animals, no pedestrians, no traffic. They were as alone as they had been. More alone because of all they were leaving behind.

The trip was uneventful to the point of boredom, filled up with inconsequential conversation meant to pass the time but not tax the intellect or imagination. A long, wearying drive back to civilization by two people who had too little and too much to say to one another. They arrived without incident and Mick let her off at her door.

"Dinner?" he asked. She shook her head. "I'm still full from that breakfast."

He said through the window, "I'll call you."

She said, "Tomorrow, please. I'm going to crash for what's left of today and all of tonight."

"Okay," he said, and pulled away. She waved. He waved back.

And then the street was empty. She unlocked the door and went in.

She unpacked, hung up her clothes, stowed her bag in the hall closet. She chose a book at random from the shelf and tried to read it, but her mind would not stay on the page. She watched the day fade to twilight outside her window, listened to the city sounds of traffic and sidewalk chatter. There was nothing in the fridge, so she ordered take-away from the shop on the corner. She was not hungry, but she hoped that dinner would return her to something like routine and help dispel the lingering unease she had brought home with her. But she hated eating from cartons, and went about setting the table with plate napkin, water glass, a candle for elegance. In spite of such civilizing trimmings, she stopped after the first mouthful. It was *mu shu* pork, and it was a mistake. The taste brought her back to the Solstice party, the ritual slice, the obligatory first bite. She felt her gorge rise, gagged, couldn't swallow, spat out the morsel. Her own body was her enemy. After long minutes during which she hung convulsed over the plate while the scene replayed itself in her memory, she recovered enough to scrape the leavings into the dustbin together with the rest of the food in the carton, and mechanically go about clearing the table, washing the dishes and putting them away. The work was calming, undemanding, purely physical.

But when the dishes were done and put away, there was nothing she wanted to do, and a great deal she wanted to not think about. The faces of Tiernon and Greenie and Lame Elly and Mick spun in her head like pinwheels and made her dizzy. She went into the bathroom and splashed cold water on her face. It looked back at her from the mirror, pale, haggard, with dark hollows under the eyes. The face of a stranger. She brushed her teeth, put on her pajamas, and piled into bed, determined to go at once to sleep.

It didn't happen. She lay in stubborn relaxation, eyes firmly shut, waiting for sleep to come and claim her like a mystery lover in a darkened room. But sleep was a wayward lover, and he declined to woo her. The harder she beckoned the less he responded. She was bone-tired, physically and mentally exhausted, emotionally drained, bereft of all will, yet she could not sleep. She didn't want to think, feel, want, be, involve herself with anything or anyone. She wanted to not want. The effort of trying to sort out the events and emotions of the past days was beyond her. She hoped it would stay that way.

Time passed.

I am a leaf floating on the surface of a lake, she told herself. *I am a cloud drifting across a blue sky. I am a kite cut loose from its string. No strings, that's me.* It was supposed to be funny, but it wasn't very, and it didn't help.

She watched the night go by, watched her window turn from black to grey to rose. *No sense just lying here, might as well get up.* She threw back the covers, stood up, felt her head spin, took two wobbly steps, lost her balance and fell down. Her phone was ringing. She could hear it as from a great distance. In another world, she thought, and slid headlong into a cave under black water.

✦ ✦ ✦

She swam up out of black water into cold white light. Around her other lights were blinking and unseen machines were making beeping noises. Through blurry eyes she saw Mick bending over her.

He said, "Hi."

"Hi" was all she could manage before sinking back into her sea-cave for another eternity. When she swam back up he was still there, but now the light was softer, and the blinking lights and the beeping noises were gone. He took her hand.

"Ow!" she said.

"Sorry. I bumped the IV. Give me the other hand."

"IV? Am I in a hospital?"

"You are. And a good thing, too. You were in bad shape. Still are."

"What time is it?"

"About nine o'clock in the evening."

"Any particular day?"

"Don't get smart with me, lady. It's the day after we came back from our ill-fated trip to fairyland."

"How did I . . . ? Did you bring me here? What happened?"

211

"I'd been ringing you since seven this morning, and got no answer, so I thought I'd better come round and check. Good thing, too. I don't know how long you'd been out, but I found you lying on the floor beside your bed about 10:00 a.m. Out like a light. Couldn't rouse you, called an ambulance, and here you are. All in a day's work."

"Thanks, chum. I seem always to be asking you 'what happened?' but in this case I really and truly don't know. I remember not being able to sleep, and getting up around dawn to go make coffee, but I guess I didn't get very far."

"I guess you didn't."

"How long am I here for?"

"They're saying a couple of days. They say you're just run-down and dehydrated, but they want to run some tests to make sure."

"I'll have to call in to work."

"I've already done that."

"Oh Mick, you are a darling. My Frog Prince. What would I do without you?"

She reached to hug him, but got tangled in a spiderweb of tubes.

"Curb your enthusiasm. I like being hugged, but you've got too many tubes coming out of you, and you're rocking the IV. Look, it's late and they're kicking all us visitors out. I'm going to leave now, and let you get some rest. You're not out of the woods yet. Just remember to be a good girl and do what they tell you."

"Mick, I will remember, and I will be a good girl."

He kissed her chastely on the forehead and took his leave.

Aftermath

After this crisis there came a curious period of stasis for both Kath and Mick, a time out of time, a border region wherein they hung suspended between past and present, real and unreal, here and there. Kath used the time to write in her journal, finding release in letting her imagination run riot while her body was bed-bound. She remained in hospital for several days, obediently following instructions, obediently swallowing a variety of pills and vitamins, forcing down a succession of tasteless but calorie-laden meals designed to build her strength and fatten her up.

"Your bones are beautiful," said Mick at the end of one lunchtime visit, "but they could use a little padding. Every time I hug you I'm afraid I'll cut myself."

She laughed shakily and promised to become fat. "And that'll teach you!" she threatened, "to be careful what you wish for."

He laughed, shakily, and promised to stop wishing.

He was with her as often as he could be, coming every day, sitting quietly by her bedside, saying little, offering himself as a presence.

The afternoon she was released from the hospital he came to get her, trundled her down to Discharge, signed the papers, made a stop at the grocer's for supplies. Arriving at her apartment building, he would have carried her up the stairs, but at that she drew the line.

"I can walk," she protested. "I'm not a baby, for heaven's sake. I'd feel too silly being carried upstairs like a parcel."

"Okay, but I'm right behind you in case you trip."

She made it to the top but slowly, using the handrail as much as the steps, and she was grateful for his hand under her elbow.

Once inside, she had to admit that Mick was impeccable. He didn't fuss over her; he didn't treat her like porcelain; he didn't insist that she go straight to bed. He stowed the groceries they'd bought in the fridge, settled her in a chair by the window, made tea, had a cup with her and filled her a second one.

"Want me to stay a while? Just to get you settled?"

She shook her head. "I'm fine, honest. And I'd like to just chill out, maybe take a nap before bedtime."

"Okay. You're home safe and relatively sound. You know I'm here if you need me. I'll look in on you tomorrow." Another chaste kiss on the forehead and he was in the doorway. Hesitating. "Sure you'll be all right?"

"I'm sure. Anything happens, I'll call you right off."

Nevertheless, when the door closed behind him and she heard his feet clattering down the stairs, she felt the silence surge back. She sat quietly, cradling the teacup between her hands. Its warmth was comforting, and she needed comfort. She drew in a deep breath and let it out. She was tired, but the days in hospital had given her some time to step back and look at events rather than struggle against them.

Now listen, Kath, she told herself. *It's time you got a handle on all this nonsense. Time to figure out what really happened. Or didn't happen. If all of that weirdness was just moonshine, if those goings-on were all in your imagination, just waking dreams, then, my dear, you are seriously off your rocker, and you need to get help. Get your head on straight. If they did happen, if what you saw and went through was real, then it's not you but your whole world that's off its rocker, and getting help is not an option because there's nothing to help.*

The prospect was terrifying. Because she knew in her gut, with her memory, with everything that made her who she was, that it was real.

I couldn't have just imagined it, she told herself. *I'm not that good. And what had happened was no formula fairy story with a fairy godmother and a prince and a happy ending. It was bad. Brutal. It out-Grimmed the Grimms at their grimmest. It was a nightmare scene from a Fuseli painting.*

But if that was the case, if there really was another terrifying reality lurking just out of range, just the other side of the ordinary world, then . . . then what? She didn't know, and there was no one who could tell her. All her teasing of Mick, all her jokes and raillery about the rushy glen and Little Bridget came back to haunt her, and at last she knew the jokes for what they were, makeshift barricades to fence out another reality, one that had been threatening all her life to claim her the minute she stopped joking and let down her guard. She was not joking now. She was profoundly disturbed, shaken to the roots of her being. If she took down the barricade, there was nothing between her and madness. For that was how everyone would see it.

Even Mick. Especially Mick, so secure and certain, enclosed within his own little shield-wall of books.

He was loving and patient, and he wanted to keep her safe, and she loved him for that.

But safe from what? From whom? Greenie? Lame Elly? Tiernon?

She forced herself to face the fact that she was her own danger. And if that were true, then it was Mick who stood between her and madness, who kept her sane simply by being what he was. The things about him that exasperated her the most, that he could joke about her fears and superstitions, that he was logical, supremely rational, unafraid of the dark, at once curious and unconvinced, were the very things that grounded her. Mick was the wall against which she lobbed her fear, the barrier that stood between her and the bogey that had threatened her all her life.

And the moral of the story is: you need Mick whether you want to or not. Probably most when you don't want to. And the other moral is: he may not need you. You drive him round the bend sometimes, just as he does you. Perfect example of opposites attracting.

She drained the last of her tea, carried her cup and saucer into the kitchen and put them in the sink, then went into the bedroom and surveyed the mess she had left behind her. The bed was a shambles, pillows tossed every which way, sheets rumpled, covers on the floor. She stripped the bed, stuffed the soiled linens in the laundry hamper, and re-made the bed with crisp, fresh sheets. Then she shucked off her creased, grimy, left-over-from-the-hospital shirt and pants and sent them to join the bedclothes, ran herself a scalding tub, poured in some scented oil and bubble bath and climbed in. Sinking deep into the water, she imagined the perturbing memories of the past days floating away with the bubbles while she soaked. She didn't get out until the water turned tepid, then toweled, slipped on a clean nightdress, and slid between cool sheets, where she slept quietly and — as far as she knew — dreamlessly throughout the night and woke refreshed into a new morning.

Being Normal

The phone ringing woke him out of sleep.

"Mick? Hi. It's me. Did I wake you?"

"You did but that's okay. What time is it, anyway?"

"It's seven a.m. Listen, love, I'm sorry to roust you out of bed, but I have something to tell you. It's important."

"What's up? You all right?"

"Yes. That's what I want to tell you. I'm all right. I'm very all right and I think I'm back to normal."

"Slow down, lady. What do you mean by 'normal'? You've been out of hospital less than one day. Are you trying to tell me you're completely recovered? Permit me some skepticism."

She laughed at that. "Mick, I will permit you all the skepticism you like. What I mean is, I'm okay. No ghosties or ghoulies or things that go bump in the night. I'm ready to live an ordinary everyday life and be glad of it. And I want to celebrate that. Will you celebrate with me? What are you doing this afternoon?"

"Well, it's Saturday. I was going to put gas in my car, do grocery shopping, run some errands. But I'll happily forego all that to celebrate you being normal, only not too normal or you'll be dull as ditchwater. What kind of normal would suit milady's fancy? Walk in the park and smell flowers? Visit the zoo and let the animals laugh at our antics? Go out to dinner? Take in a show? You name it, I'm your man."

"I'd like to do all of the above but not all at once. I'll settle for a walk in the park and dinner. I've got to get my place in order, do laundry, pick up the pieces of my life. Why don't you come by at about teatime, we'll have a cup, go for a walk, and wind up in some cozy restaurant for a lovely dinner."

That evening set the tone. They stayed to safe topics—rigged elections, political and sexual scandals, revolutions in various parts of the world. Neither mentioned hospitals, fainting spells, dreams, country lore or seasonal myths. They walked on eggs and none got broken. It was the first of many such evenings — walks in the park, dinners in quiet restaurants, cautious companionship and carefully orchestrated good times designed to override the recent past for both of them. Kath's normality became the running joke that carried them. When conversation faltered they fell back on their Kath Is Crazy act.

"Mick? I feel an attack of normality coming on. Can we go dancing in the rain in our underwear? Or shoot out some streetlights after midnight?"

It was his cue and he picked it up. "You'd better watch out, Kath. These attacks of normal are becoming dangerously frequent. Next thing you'll find yourself joining a Book Club. Or taking up golf. A little normality is a dangerous thing."

"Dancing in the rain is a good antidote. Keeps you fit and clean and close to nature all at the same time."

On such badinage summer slid into autumn, the weather cooled, evenings grew darker, nights grew longer. October came and went, and then November, the dark time of the year. The Winter Solstice was approaching, and both Mick and Kath were aware of it though neither said so. One dining-out evening, Mick sprang his secret. When they were at their usual table and had ordered drinks, he casually pulled from his briefcase and placed in the space between them a journal, *Folkways and Folklore*. He left her to read the table of contents, watching for the look on her face.

He got it, and more besides, as she read aloud, "'Tradition and the Individual Talent: Lame Elly and the Grally Tusker,' by Dr. Michael McKennan. Mick, you sneak! You never told me! All this time you've had this in the works!"

"I've been saving it for the right time. And this is it."

"And *Folkways and Folklore*! That's top of the tree, isn't it? The best. Why didn't you tell me?" She flipped the pages, found his article, read the first sentences aloud. "'It isn't so much what she says as how she says it.' You're right there. A good way to start." She went on. "'Lame Elly, blind yet gifted with inner vision, became the Grally Tusker as she unfolded his tale, and from her one-room cottage lit by fire, scented with driftwood smoke and filled with eager listeners, we were transported to a dark wood, a deserted castle, and an enchanted banquet-table where an extraordinary drama unfolded before our eyes.' Some nice detail there. You've got the atmosphere. 'Before our eyes is not a figure of speech, dear reader. We saw what she spoke. And felt it. The challenge for the pedestrian folklorist reporting this phenomenon is how to capture art in cold print, how to re-present, on the silent page, a uniquely oral performance. I want to say the storyteller possessed the story. But it would be closer to the truth to say the story possessed her, took her over and told itself through her.'"

She put the book down. "Mick, that's a wonderful opening. You're a pretty good storyteller yourself. You've hit just the right note, caught the ambience." Her excitement seemed genuine, her approval unfeigned, untainted by memories. "I want to read the whole thing. Can I have a copy?"

Mick tried not to look as relieved as he felt. It hadn't disturbed her, hadn't stirred up old experience. She really was okay.

"Yes, you can have a copy. This one's for you; that's why I brought it. And there's more news." He made a stab at looking modest, but missed by a mile. "This is just the first chapter of my book. I signed the contract yesterday. It's scheduled to come out next fall."

"A whole book? Mick, that's terrific! And you just out of grad school! You'll be the youngest folklore scholar in history. What are you going to call it? Don't go all stodgy with something dull and academic with a colon and a subtitle."

"Give me a break, will you? I don't like those dry-as-dust thesis titles any more than you do. Put the reader off altogether, I should think. I'm thinking of calling it *Stories That Tell Themselves*. No colon, no subtitle. What do you think?"

She put down the journal and looked at him. "I think it's just right. Perfect. I'd buy a book like that in a heartbeat. Congratulations, Mick. Here's to you."

She raised her glass in a toast, and he clinked it with his. She went on.

"So you did it after all. You nailed your undiscovered story-teller and you got what you went for." A thought struck her. "Mick, don't you have to get permission or give the story-tellers program credit or something? Can you just retell the stories?"

"Of course I got permission. I couldn't publish without it. Give me some credit, will you? Elly's blind, so I wrote to the guy, you know, Tiernon. I explained what I was doing and sent a note to be signed. And he sent it back. All correct, so don't worry."

"Then are you going to send them a copy? The faery folk?"

"The who?"

"You know. Lame Elly. And Tiernon and Greenie."

"That gang? What's 'faery' about them? They seem pretty earthy to me. A bit out of the way, maybe, but otherwise ordinary."

"It's just an expression. Goes with that gingerbread cottage where they had the gab. But you do owe them, I think."

"Not them. Her. Lame Elly. And I did send her a copy. Inscribed. Empty courtesy, really, since she's blind. But maybe somebody will read it to her. Now let's forget the faery folk, shall we? They're there, and we're here. Ready to order?"

She looked at him narrowly. "Mick, are you worried about me? You don't have to be. I'm normal, remember? I'm okay, Mick. Really okay."

"I'll take your word for it. In that case, are you ready for a shock? I found out what Grally means. It's dialect, of course. But it's a real word, and I actually give it a footnote. You'll never guess."

"Go ahead. Shock me."

"It means worthy, proper, seemly, comely (of a woman), handsome (of a man). Can you beat it? The Seemly Tusker. The Handsome Tusker. Go figure."

She considered it seriously, head on one side.

"So Beauty is the Beast. Well, you know, it makes sense in a way. He'd have to be something special. And to be seemly or handsome instead of ugly or grotesque would make him even more scary. To me, anyway. Like those sexy vampires that are all the rage. Beauty and terror all wrapped up in one package."

The waiter was hovering, and, to Mick's relief, Kath changed the subject.

"Enough about all that. Let's get to the important things. Like food. Yes, I'm ready to order. I'll have the garlic snails to start. And then the boeuf bourguignon and asparagus vinaigrette. Fraises de bois with crème fraiche for dessert. And espresso to finish."

She grinned at Mick. "It's your turn to pay."

Patterns of an Older Story

The year passed. The Winter Solstice went by, carefully unremarked by either of them. Christmas came and went with gifts and decorations. Having seen the New Year in at a small party of friends, mostly Mick's academic crowd, they were walking back to Kath's place in the small hours of New Year's Day. The night was frosty and clear and the city lights were no competition for the cold constellations that looked down on them, patterns of an older story. Although he had not planned it two seconds before he spoke, Mick chose that moment to propose.

"You know what I think? I think we should get married."

Kath stopped walking, and for a moment he was afraid she was going to laugh. But she didn't. Instead she smiled, and tilted her head to look into his eyes. "Are you sure Mick? Because we don't have to. I'm perfectly happy with things the way they are."

"I'm not," he said, and the sharpness of his tone made her blink. "You're my 'bird,' remember? But you're too flighty for my comfort, and you could take wing at any minute. I'm no demon lover, but I need to have you tethered to your perch."

"But marriage isn't a tether. Or a perch. At least, it ought not to be either. It should be a partnership. That's what I've always thought. Hoped."

"Okay, you're right, a partnership. No tether, no perch. Will you be my partner?"

"With all the rigmarole? In sickness and in health? Richer and poorer and all that?"

"All the rigmarole. Whatever comes. For the long voyage. I mean it, Kath."

They were stopped under a streetlamp, two people enclosed in a little cone of light carved out of the dark, alone in their private world.

"Mick, my darling heart, I know you mean it. But I'm not sure you ought to. I'm usually the fool who rushes in, but for once it's my turn to be cautious. Do you know what you're letting yourself in for? I have a terrible tendency to go off the deep end, as you well know. Sure you don't want to change your mind?"

"Too late," he said. "I'm not going to change my mind. I understand why you're hesitating. And that's just why I'm rushing in."

She started to speak, but he put his finger to her lips.

"I know what you're like, and that's why I want you tied. That way, if you do go off the deep end, I'll be holding onto the other end of the rope. Let's drop the metaphors. I want us to be a team, to go home together, to make the most of the good times and help each other over the rough places."

Then she was silent for so long he began to be afraid of what she might say, and then was afraid to break the silence. They walked on, neither speaking. The streets were quiet with no traffic. Their footfalls in the clear cold air were the only sound to disturb the night. The stars were waiting. They arrived at her door and she fished the front door key out of her purse and handed it to him.

"Okay," she said. "I mean . . . yes."

He unlocked her door, and together they went in and up the stairs.

✦ ✦ ✦

Decision taken, the whole operation was accomplished with a minimum of fuss. A civil ceremony at the Registry Office, a wedding lunch for two, and some logistical adjustments in housekeeping. The weather helped. An unusually bright spring brought early-blooming flowers, trees leafing out ahead of schedule, a warm and genial atmosphere that encouraged enterprise and made adventure easy.

They decided to honor their new state by finding newer and bigger accommodations than either of them had had. Combining incomes, they leased the first and second floors of a tall old house on a square, newly renovated and divided into apartments. An open-plan sitting room on the first floor ran the length of the house with a kitchen-dining area at the far end and a door to the back terrace. A hall stairway led up to two bedrooms and bath upstairs. Long windows front and back were designed to catch the breeze. The terrace off the kitchen had flower borders, a gnarled apple tree and a lilac whose scent drifted in the bedroom window on warm evenings. Across the narrow road in front, a blackbird sang in the little square.

They pooled their furniture to achieve an eclectic decor of hand-me-down and thrift shop. Kath bought a scattering of cushions in all colors to "pull things together," and put up pictures— seascapes, landscapes, and a cherished, tattered clown poster from a childhood trip to the circus. A second-hand kitchen table covered with ten coats of chipped and flaking paint came cheap, and for two weekends Mick scraped and sanded. The table turned out to be solid walnut, and rubbing with oil brought out the grain. Their combined books took up all four walls of the second bedroom, which they were already rather self-consciously calling "the library." A special space on the crowded shelves was reserved for *Stories That Tell Themselves* when it came out.

Housekeeping sorted itself out. They did the marketing and the laundry together; when they were tired of takeaway they made dinner turnabout, each contributing favorite dishes. Mick's specialty was spaghetti with sauce Bolognese, Kath's was coq au vin. They traded the cooking and washing-up, and found that Saturday cleaning went faster with two sharing. Even making the bed took half the time with someone on either side. Neither of them had great expectations, and the fact that they began to enjoy the partnership came as a surprise to both of them. Kath was astonished at how easy it seemed, and Mick allowed himself to hope that being married might actually work. They were, in fact, happy, but they were too busy to notice.

"I feel like I'm playing house," Kath told him over bed-making one day. "This is too much fun to be real." She fluffed up a pillow.

"Who says reality can't be fun?" he countered, and threw its mate at her. "There's got to be some justification for it."

Banter became the hallmark of their relationship, a pattern of light repartee skimming them across the surface of marriage. In those early months such banter did much to smooth the rough spots that any two people encounter when the dynamic in a relationship changes.

"Figure skating," said Kath to herself.

"Thin ice," thought Mick. But so far it seemed to be holding.

Until one day . . .

"Mick, have a look at this."

He read the headline over her shoulder. "'Folklore or Fakelore? Prehistoric Spirals Pecked into Stone Sites Now Thought to be Modern Fakes to Draw Tourists.'"

"What do you think of that?"

"It'll put the antiquarians in an uproar. We'll have to wait for the dust to settle."

"I don't care about the antiquarians. I don't believe they're fakes. Not all of them, anyway. There were spirals in the cliff wall by Lame Elly's cottage. A right-hand one and a left-hand one. I told you. They were overgrown with vines, but Tiernon said they were put there ages ago. When I saw them first, I had the oddest feeling that I knew them. I'd like to see them again."

They were edging into dangerous territory. She wanted to explore it. He didn't.

"Honey, right now the last thing I want to talk about is fake folklore. It's been a long day, and I'm tired and hungry. Let's go out to dinner."

"But it's my turn to cook."

"I'll give you the night off. We deserve someone else's cooking. I'm in the mood for something highly spiced and indigestible. Foong Lin's Mexican Tandoori Pizza. How about you?"

"You certainly know how to change the subject. Okay. If we're going gourmet I want garlic ice cream with mushroom sauce for dessert."

"You got it, lady. Let's go. Grab your coat and get your hat. Leave your worries on the doorstep. We're stepping out with Fred and Ginger."

✦ ✦ ✦

Settling her into a booth, he kept up the banter. "Looks like the menu doesn't have my favorite item tonight—roasted raspberries with clam sauce. We'll have to settle for watery gruel and coffee Oliver Twist—if you ask for more they show you the door."

The joke was feeble, but his audience was receptive and eager to be amused.

She relaxed against the banquette and giggled. "That's good. And good for me. I haven't been really silly and childish for ages. All work and no play makes Jill a dull pill. And makes Kath a real meth. And makes Mick a . . ."

"Keep it clean."

Their high lasted through the salad (Caesar), the entrée (Mediterranean chicken) and dessert (Crème Brulé with red raspberries). But when the coffee came the fun was over. Kath poured sugar from the packet, dropped in the twist of lemon, stirred, drained the cup and set it down with a clack.

"Now. What are you thinking that you're not telling me? I can't read your mind, but I can read your face, and It's full of unsaid things."

"If you must know, I'm concerned about that story in the paper."

"Well, I just thought it was an interesting coincidence."

"I can read your face too, and what I see in it is more than coincidence. That story is stirring up things I was hoping we'd buried. I don't want to dig them up again."

"Oh for heaven's sake. It's just a newspaper story. It'll be in tomorrow's trash."

"Talk all you want to about tomorrow's trash, but if it reminds you of some things that I for one would like to forget—and you should too—then it isn't tomorrow's trash, it's today's problem. I don't know if those spirals are real or fake and I don't care. I do care about you and what happened to you up there. And what's happening to you now. Because you want to go back, don't you?"

A pause.

"Well, yes. I'd like to have another look. They're mysterious, and I like mysteries. They beg to be solved. But I don't see why that's so terrible. I only saw them that once."

She picked up her coffee cup, made to drink, saw there were only dregs and put it down again. He signaled the waiter for the check.

"We could just look at them without telling anyone we were there," she continued. "I don't want to renew old acquaintance any more than you do, or go through a lot of 'hello-how-are-yous' with people we'll never see again. I agree that some things are better left buried, and I certainly don't want to dig them up."

Oh yes you do, he thought. *That's exactly what you want, but you can't admit that even to yourself.* He knew better than to say it, so he tried a joke. "Born to trouble as the sparks fly upward, that's Kath."

"What do you mean, 'that's Kath?' What's Kath? Who said that?"

"Job said it. In the Bible. 'Man is born to trouble as the sparks fly upward.' Nice image. Poor old Job wasn't looking for trouble but trouble found him anyway. As it does most people. But you, Kath, you go Job one better. You don't go looking for trouble; you dream it up." He knew before the words had died that he'd made a mistake. He felt the temperature drop from mild to freezing in micro-seconds, a change so fast he couldn't keep pace with it.

"Oh, is that what I do? Dream it up? Thank you very much for telling me; I might not have known otherwise. And you're Mr. Sane and Sober all set to wake me up. Where would I be without you, Mick? A lot you know about it. You don't believe that anything happened."

He was caught in a hurricane, blown sideways by the suddenness and force of her attack. His joke had misfired, but her reaction was out of proportion, a volcano erupting out of a coffee cup. Something else was going on. What he'd meant as playful had touched a nerve. With fatal good intentions he'd said exactly the wrong thing and it was too late now to take it back, too late even to get in a word edgewise. She was off and running.

"Up on your high horse, aren't you, Mick? You always know best, don't you? You know better than everybody else, don't you? Your judgment is the right one. Always."

The sentences came like cannon shot, and the sudden ferocity of her attack left him breathless. The fire had blazed up from nowhere so quick and hot it was out of control already. She was more than angry—she was furious. There was a red flush across her cheekbones and her eyes were bright with angry tears. He jumped into her pause for breath.

"I'm sorry. I didn't mean it that way. It was just a joke. I thought you'd laugh."

"I don't think it's funny. I don't think I'm funny. I show you a really interesting newspaper item and right away you get all psychological and start analyzing things you know nothing about. Well, Mr. Superior, if you think I'm so born to trouble, why don't you bail out and leave me to my fate? I was doing just fine without you."

She grabbed her purse, slid out of the booth, and was headed for the door before he could catch up. When he reached for her arm, she shook him off, and there was a stupid and embarrassing tussle in the doorway before she broke free, and almost running, was halfway down the street not even looking where she was going. He caught her up at the corner, when the blessed traffic light turned red just in time.

"Kath will you for God's sake wait a minute? I'm really sorry. I apologize."

She stared straight ahead, waiting for the light to change.

"Kath, please."

Silence.

He tried another joke. "We can't keep on fighting in the street like this. We'll spook the horses."

At that he got a grudging smile and breathed a sigh of relief.

"Pax? Can we declare a truce? At least for right now?"

"All right. Pax," she agreed. "Truce for right now."

And he took her arm, and the light turned green, and they crossed the street with the shadow of the fight between them. It was not over, and they knew it.

Truce

What they called truce was a state of affairs as brittle as glass and as easy to see through, revealing their whole brief married life to have been as fragile as a stained glass window in a war zone. They both knew that the wrong word could shatter everything, could open a crack between them so wide they might never be able to find their way back to each other across it. Each was terrified by that possibility. Each was certain of being in the right. Each was wary of provoking the other's unreasonable reaction.

All next day they were at stalemate, carefully playing out a charade of ordinary life, carefully pretending nothing was wrong, each waiting for the other to make the first move. The worst of it was they could only keep the peace by being polite to each other, and the falsity was chilling. Civility and good manners gave them a surface on which to skate, but just beneath and darkening the ice was the deep water of their first serious quarrel since getting married. It scared both of them so badly they were afraid to acknowledge their fear.

It was Mick's turn to cook. He went grocery-shopping, hoping the market would give him a dinner idea that would heal the breach. He roamed up and down the aisles, dodging women pushing loaded carts, narrowly missing the occasional child staring at candy bars, or teen loading up on soft drinks. He found himself in the produce section looking at garlic bulbs nested between the lettuce and the endive. *Garlic to ward off evil*, he thought wryly. *Maybe Pliny was right. Folklore ought to be good for something*. He thumbed a good hard head with tightly packed cloves and the feel of it gave him inspiration. He grabbed a shopping basket, dropped the garlic in, added a selection of fresh mushrooms, velvet white with tightly closed caps, included a bunch of shallots, headed for the meat department to get a pound of beef round, and half a pound of pork loin, topped them off with a can of plum tomatoes, a box of spaghetti noodles and a half pint of cream, and crowned the lot with a head of curly dark green lettuce. A long, brown-crusted loaf of bread came next, and some deep yellow butter. At the last minute he added a bunch of windflowers, yellow and white and purple, tied with string. He paid for the lot, and with the grocery bag full went to the vintners next door and bought a straw-covered jug of Chianti.

In spite of worry about Kath, he was happy with his loot. It was good to be doing something real with tangible things. *Stick with reality, Mick,* he counseled himself, *and give imagination a rest for a while.* Arriving home, he nearly stepped on a padded mailing envelope propped against the front door. Setting down his grocery bags, he picked it up, knowing already what it was. His book. Addressed to him, with a note inside from the publisher: *With our compliments, proud to send the first copy* – etc. etc. He put the book on the table for later sharing with Kath and went straight through to the kitchen to unload. Setting out the parcels on the counter, he planned the dinner: start the sauce early, let it simmer long and slow, put the spaghetti water on to boil at the last minute and pour the wine at the same time.

He found a jug and filed it with water for the windflowers, put them in the center of the table. He drew the cork on the Chianti, splashed some into a tumbler and set it on the sink ledge, tied a tea towel around his waist and lifted down the heavy iron saucepan. He opened the can of plum tomatoes, dumped them into the pan, and set a low flame underneath. He reached in the utensil drawer for the masher and jammed it down on the tomatoes, stirring and mashing as the sauce began to bubble.

Feelings were bubbling too, and the top feeling was anger long suppressed. They were friends as well as lovers, weren't they? You'd think he was some annoying stranger instead of her husband. He grabbed the wooden chopping board by the neck, took a knife worn to concavity from many sharpenings, broke off two garlic cloves and peeled and minced them with angry precision. He pulverized a generous pinch of oregano between thumb and palm, added half a pinch of thyme, stirred both into the sauce with a sprinkle of sea salt, stirred in the minced garlic, added a generous squeeze of tomato paste, covered the whole tightly with a heavy lid and turned the flame low to simmer. He set butter and olive oil to melt in the frypan while he peeled and chopped fine the onion, celery and carrot scraped it all into the sizzle, diced the beef and pork into small cubes. When the vegetables began to brown, he added the meat a cube or two at a time. *I've put up with a lot from you, you know. You think it's easy watching you chase will o' the wisps? Think it's fun watching you wear yourself out? And picking up the pieces afterward?*

He had forgotten his wine. The first sip was cool and fresh and tasted faintly of summer fruit. He took a larger swallow and set it on the counter near to hand. The meat was browning nicely. He pushed the vegetables to one side so they would not overcook, turned the meat to brown with his favorite wooden spoon, rapping it smartly on the side of the pan to stop the drips. He turned up the heat. He gave the tomato sauce a stir, ladled up a spoonful, sipped it experimentally. *Too bland.* He added a pinch more salt, sipped again. *Still a bit new.* A splash of wine and a quick stir. *Give it a couple more hours.*

The smell of sautéing meat was beginning to blend with the rich aroma of frying onion and the sharp-sweet tang of tomatoes on the simmer. Quickly he peeled and sliced the mushrooms, stirred them in to the sauce. When they were ready, he scraped the sautéed meat and onion and their attendant juices into the tomato sauce, poured in the cream, lowered the heat under the pot, fitted the lid tightly. The salad would come last. Nothing to do now but wait.

He heard her key in the lock.

"Mick? I thought this was your seminar night."

"It was. I cancelled class. Kath, about what happened—"

They both spoke at once.

"I'm sorry—"

"I'm sorry—"

They stopped, started over.

"Mick I'm so sorry I blew up at you the other night. I don't know what happened. I was on edge and I . . . I guess you just pushed a button. Forgive and forget?"

He took both her hands, led her into the front room, sat her down.

"I'm sorry too, for needling you the way I did. And yes of course, forgive. But not forget. Not yet. We're killing each other with care. You

249

know what I mean. Can we please find a way to clear the air so we can be easy again?"

No reply, but a look of such resignation that it scared him.

"We need to talk things through, but we surely can find a way to do it without hurting each other. Can't we?"

Then she answered. "No, I don't think we can. Because we'll be taking about different things. We don't mix well, Mick. We're oil and water, though which of us is which I don't know."

"It doesn't matter. And if we can't mix, maybe we can match, find a place to meet. As long as we stay with what's important."

"But that's just it. What's important to me is just 'dreams' to you. And it's important to you to explain away everything that's really important to me. Stories are alive to me. They're just data to you." She decided to take the plunge. "Mick, ever since last summer when we went on your story-hunting expedition you've been acting like everything that happened up there was just some aberration peculiar to me. Just dreams. Kath and her overactive imagination, wanting the leprechaun and the crock of gold."

He started to speak but she held up her hand to cut him off.

"I'm not sure what did happen up there, and I don't know yet how to make sense of it, and I'm glad you got us away when you did, because I think we were both scared. But I was scared about what was happening, and you were scared that I'd gone crazy. And something was happening, and I wasn't crazy."

He said nothing, and she continued.

"But it wasn't just me. You were there. You don't want to admit it, but you were. You saw me, and I saw you. So I won't stand for being type-cast as some psycho-freak you have to keep from getting into trouble, and I won't let you hide behind that. Whatever happened, you were part of it. The folklore captured the folklorist. The tables were turned, and the biter got bit."

He grinned ruefully. "You sound almost glad I got bit."

"I am. I'd like something to bite you hard enough to get your attention, to make you see what I see, feel what I feel. Some day that's going to dawn on you, Mick, and I hope I'm around when it does. I just hope it doesn't happen too late."

She took a deep breath. "I think that's enough to start with. Your turn."

"Okay. For the sake of argument, let's assume I'm wrong and you're right. We are caught in a story that somebody else is telling. Even if that's the case, we don't have to go along with it. We are independent people. We can guide our own lives."

Kath studied her plate, fiddled with a fork, looked up, looked down. "I'm scared."

"You don't have to be. We're neither one of us angry any more. It's okay."

"I don't mean that. I'm not scared of you, or for us—well—only a little. I'm frightened about whatever went on up there, and why it was me. Because I did fit in. And ever since, I've spent a lot of time not thinking about it. Which only makes it worse."

"I can help you not think about it."

"No you can't. That's just the trouble. That's what we've been trying to do, and it hasn't worked. The more I don't think about it, the more it's in my mind. The farther I run away the closer I get. I need to exorcise it."

"Well I'm fresh out of bell, book, and candle right now, but—"

"Please don't joke. You know what I mean."

"Sorry. Well then, if running away brings you closer, maybe coming closer will have the opposite effect. Law of inverse ratio inverted. Do you want to go back?"

"No. Yes. I don't and I do. I'm scared of opening things up again. But I can't just walk away. It's like stopping a mystery story halfway through. I want the answer. I want it solved."

"Then we should go back."

"Oh, Mick, do you mean it? Can we? I thought for sure you'd say no."

The swiftness with which she jumped on his offer was revealing. This was what she'd wanted, had been wanting all along, the hidden wish beneath her words.

"I want it solved too. We have to find a way to clear things up so we can start living again. I miss you. And I'd like to think that you miss me."

"I miss you something awful."

"Then we'll do it. How about next weekend? It's bank holiday, so it'll be a long weekend."

"The sooner the better, for me."

"I don't know exactly what we'll do up there . . ."

"We don't have to know. We can just let things unfold. Like a story when you don't know the end."

It was at that precise moment that a pungent, acrid smell attacked his nostrils.

O god, the Bolognese!

Smoke was billowing from the kitchen like a fire on an oil rig. He snatched the flaming pan off the heat, turned off the burner. Too late. The sauce was burned to the pan, a scorched and bubbling black tar. He opened the window as wide as it would go, and set the pan in the sink, where it smoldered sullenly. The air began slowly to clear, and the pan to cool. He filled it with cold water and left the disaster to soak, hoping that though the sauce was ruined the pan might not be beyond salvage.

He looked at Kath and she at him. They both laughed. Decision taken; they were both giddy with relief. They were okay. No harm except to the saucepan.

"Pizza from the takeaway?"

"Pizza from the takeaway."

Afterward they spent a couple of hours scrubbing the smoke-dirtied kitchen and treating Mick's favorite saucepan for third-degree burns.

✦ ✦ ✦

That night in bed, Kath dreamed. She knew perfectly well she was dreaming, *and that makes it safe*, she told her sleeping self. *If I know I'm dreaming I can wake up anytime I want.* She was sitting in a boat, a cockleshell craft that rode the water like a cork, dancing up one wave and down the next, always in movement, always in the same place. She could see the boat and herself in it from where she stood on the cliff, looking out. The person in the boat with her was an old friend, familiar and comfortable, and when he pointed out to her that the cockle-boat was dissolving in the seawater, she told him that was all right. They would float on the waves. *"Like sea gulls,"* she told him. *"No,"* he said, *"we'll swim."* That frightened her, and she decided to wake up, but the boat was gone, and the waves were splashing against her face, and she didn't want to open her eyes. *"Here,"* said the friend. *"Take hold of my arm. I'll hold you up."* But when she took his arm, he sank down, pulling her with him to where it was deep and green and cool, and she could see him through the greenness. Her hair floated out around her like seaweed and became a forest of groping branches that reached for her as she ran. A voice said, *"It has to will have happened,"* and a sea-branch curled around her and she stumbled and fell.

With her waking, the dream dissolved, and the harder she tried to hold it, the quicker it melted until she lost it altogether. She heard Mick gently snoring next to her, and she curled under the covers and went back to sleep. As far as she knew, she had no more dreams that night.

Treasure Hunting

Next day they set out early. The weather held; the sun shone on their happiness. Another fine day. The journey by car was faster than by coach, and they were at the hotel and checked into their room by early afternoon. They unpacked, arranged toothbrushes and toiletries, then went exploring. The town was full of little shops, and they tried to hit every one.

"Maybe we'll stumble across a copy of that book," said Kath with unexpected nostalgia.

"Titled simply, *That Book*? Or can you be more specific?"

"Mick, you cynic, how could you forget? The book that brought us together that day in Special Collections."

"*Popular Antiquities.* Do you know, I'd forgotten all about it?"

"And it was so important. One of these days you'll forget all about me."

He laid his hand over his heart. "I solemnly swear to never forget all about you Kath. Ever since that day you've been my Special Collection. So don't go and get yourself lost in Repairs."

"I won't get lost if you won't forget me. Deal?"

"Deal."

They shook hands on the bargain.

"Wouldn't it be funny if you found the book now. Let's go looking. Maybe we'll find it."

They looked, but didn't find it. Nevertheless, they found other treasures, and coffee at the hotel saw them gloating over their spoils. Kath's prize was a volume of Jenkyn Thomas's *Welsh Fairy Book* with illustrations by Willy Pogány.

"I loved this book when I was a kid," she told Mick. "He has a strange quality, Pogány, realistic and stylized all at once. See this one of the fay in the pool combing her hair and the King's son with his arms stretched out to her? That's my favorite. I love her hair. When I was a kid and haunting the library I used to pick books by their illustrations, and as a rule of thumb it never let me down. Nobody wastes a good artist on a bad book."

"It's a sound business principle," he agreed. He was clutching his own prize, a copy of Keightley's *Fairy Mythology*, half-calf, gold-stamped, and at a bargain price.

"I've been looking for this for a couple of years," he told Kath, "though not for the illustration, even if it is Cruikshank. The copy in the university library was a wreck, spine mended with tape and pages coming loose. Somebody had stolen the frontispiece and somebody else (maybe the same vandal) had written in the margins. This one's in surprisingly good condition. Maybe I'll donate it to the library. No, maybe I won't. It deserves better treatment than it would get from some borrowers. I hate it when people mistreat books."

They clinked glasses and tucked in.

After lunch they set off in the car, neither wanting to acknowledge that the day might hold hidden peril. Neither said anything when they took the much-travelled cliff road, but both knew where they were going. The sun was shining, the breeze off the sea was gentle, and the air seemed full of promise as they bowled along. The road was almost bare of traffic, and the trees seemed to have been pruned or cut back from the road. They did not crowd the travelers as they had on their previous journey, and through them Kath and Mick caught tantalizing glimpses of sun sparkling off the little wavelets of a dark green ocean.

"Look, Mick! There's the sea. What is it about the sea that changes everything so? It's exciting just to see it. Something about coming to the very edge of the land, I suppose. A boundary, a jumping-off place." She chanted:

> "Sea bites land
> as land bars sea;
> that for you
> and this for me."

"What's that?"

"Dunno. I just remembered it. I suppose I read it somewhere. In a kid's book, probably. It's one of those rhymes you find in fairy tales, like 'Flounder, flounder in the sea . . .' or 'Fee, fi, fo, fum.' They're embedded in the stories like fossils in rock, but you get the feeling they're much older. Like 'Grally.' This one actually makes more sense than most. The sea wears at the land, the land holds back the sea. Where they meet is where adventure begins. Like the road we're on. Can you feel it?"

"Well, the air is different. I can feel that. Fresher, colder. And there's a tang of salt. I like it."

"I do too. We should be in a convertible with the top down so we could really be a part of it."

"Wouldn't a convertible with the top down make your hair all windblown and stuff? Besides, a closed car is a lot safer. If we rolled in a convertible—"

"We'd roll right into the sea and turn into selkies. Use your imagination."

"I am using my imagination. I'm imagining what would be left of us if we rolled from one of these cliffs right into the sea. Unless of course we rolled inland. Let's pretend we're in a convertible and be glad we're in a nice safe car. Besides, we're nearly there. Remember the woods? And the humpbacked bridge and all? Time to leave the car where we can find it, right by the road."

The banter was over, its purpose, to mask anxiety, accomplished and discarded. He pulled over and parked. They were there. He leaned across her and opened the door. They started down the path.

"Look out, Elfland! Here we come!" She drew in a deep breath and exhaled memory. Like a double exposure photograph, Kath felt superimposed on her past self.

She stretched out an arm for steadiness, and her fingers brushed a pattern. There were light, regular indentations in the rock.

She heard Tiernon's voice behind her. "They're from the long ago time."

She pulled her hand away and turned to him, but it was Mick behind her. In sudden panic she reached for the safety of his hand, held it in both hers.

"Mick, let's go back. I'm afraid. I don't want to do this."

Mick was insistent. "I think you'd better stick with the plan," he said. "You've come this far. Don't back out now. Show me what's there."

Moments passed while he waited. At last she nodded. Holding his hand, she guided his index finger around the curves and re-curves of the right-hand maze.

"That's the path to the center," she told him. "That's the path I followed."

"Fine. You've reconnected with your memories. That's what we came for." He tried to be easy and unhurried, not to sound as anxious as he felt. "By the time we get back to the hotel, it'll be time for dinner. I don't know about you, but I'm hungry, and I want a shower and a change of clothes after crashing through all those brambles on the path."

"Can't we go a little farther? I'd like to see the cottage again, maybe say hello to Elly."

He looked at her face, eager and ready to take whatever came, and inside himself he said *she won't even know she is giving in until it is too late*. But to her he said, "Okay. A quick 'hello,' and then we're the hell out of here." He walked beside and a little in front of her as they continued down the path, and he gripped her hand hard.

After the deep shade of the path the afternoon sun reflecting off the water as they emerged made it hard to see for a moment. The door opened and a grizzled man in a worn-at-elbows green jacket stood peering out, sun-blind after the dark interior. It was Tiernon, from the gab and the Solstice party but his dark-accustomed vision could not see who was there.

"Who is it, then?"

A voice behind him said, "Kath, is it? And Mick?"

Tiernon stood aside as Kath said, "Greenie."

Greenie blinked and stared at them both. "The pair of you! Are you here for the gab?"

Tiernon said, "You're a bit early. It's tonight. Come back about sundown, we'll be ready then." He nodded to Kath and Mick as he eased past them in the doorway on his way out. Greenie said "Come in, come in."

Mick said, "No, really, we shouldn't. We just stopped by to say hello."

"Nonsense. Of course come in. We're that glad to see you, just surprised, you know how it is. You'll stay for the gab and welcome, I hope. It's tonight, as Tiernon says. But a cup of tea while you're here? Don't just stand there, you two. Come in and be easy."

Feeling like intruders, Mick and Kath surrendered to her insistence, and came, their eyes still blinded by the sunlight, into a room full of shadows. While Greenie put the kettle on, they stood looking around, remembering their first visit, the crowded room, the haze of smoke.

"You'll find it much the same, my dears, just without so many people," said a voice, reading their minds.

Peering through the gloom, Kath saw a familiar white-haired woman seated in a low chair by the fireplace.

"Come here to me," said Lame Elly, and with relief Kath left the table and crossed to where Elly sat by the fire. She pulled up a little three-legged stool and sat. Elly said no word, but reached sightlessly for Kath's hand, and Kath slid her fingers into the cool, papery, firm grip of the old woman.

"You're all right," said Elly. "It isn't finished."

They sat in silence, hand in hand. Kath heard the voices of Greenie and Mick, words without meaning rising and falling, weaving a lattice of colored sound around which the silence curled like the tendril of a vine.

From a great distance Kath heard herself say. "What must I do?"

"You'll know," said Elly.

Manners Be Damned

After a decent interval they took their leave, promising in response to much insistence that they would return that evening for the gab.

"But I'm not sure that's a good idea," said Mick as they drove away. "Not twice in one day. You'll be tired," he told Kath.

"Mick, we have to go. They practically ordered us to be there, and it would be rude to have them know we're here and not to attend. You're the one who told me to mind my manners, way last summer."

"Manners be damned. It's your welfare I'm thinking about."

"Mick, you are my darling, and you take wonderful care of me, and I love you for it, but honestly my welfare is faring well—pretty well, I hope. I'm okay and I wish you wouldn't worry so."

He thought, *You will not be okay until I get you the hell away from here, and you are making that harder for both of us every minute*. Aloud he said, "We didn't come up here to get dragged into another ritual. And it's not like we're essential. The gab will happen whether we're there or not."

"But there'll be stories, won't there? Isn't that what this is all about? You'd have a legitimate reason to be there. You might even tell a story yourself."

They made the rest of the drive in silence.

Kath broke first. "Mick. Please let's not go back to being polite with each other. I'll tell you what I think and you can tell me what you think. Okay?"

"Right. You start."

"Well, when we came up here I felt like it was unfinished business. Like there was something special we had to do."

"And you think you can finish it by going to the gab? Is that what you and Elly were talking about while I was being polite with Greenie? Close as twins you were."

"I didn't think you noticed. I didn't think you were paying any attention."

"I always pay attention to you and what you're doing. But Greenie was talking, and I couldn't hear you."

"We hardly said two words to each other, really. Elly took my hand, because she saw — I mean she sensed — that I was upset. All she said was 'It isn't finished.' I said 'What must I do?' and she said, 'You'll know.' And that's all she said. And that's why I really want to be there tonight. Because maybe that's when I'll know. When I can finish whatever's unfinished and get done with it once and for all."

He reached across the table and took both her hands, cradled them in his own, warm and enveloping.

"My darling heart, that is the biggest load of crap I've heard in a long time. All those cryptic sentences — It isn't finished — You'll know — they sound portentous because they're short and declarative. And you're falling for it. Kath, Kath listen to me. You don't have to do anything. Don't get sucked into this."

"I'm sucked in already, Mick. I am a part of whatever's going on whether I want to be or not. I didn't know that when we decided to come back here. Honestly. But now I do know it. And I have to be."

He gave up, shrugged, said, "All right, Kath. We'll go to the gab and we'll listen to the stories. But afterward, when it's over, will you let me take you home? Wherever that is?"

The Road

"I'm going to miss this road when we finally get back home," said Kath. "It feels like an old acquaintance."

But even as she said the words, her voice dropped and she fell silent. The road was strange in its familiarity. It was not the same cheerful road they had travelled in daylight that morning. Rather, it was the same haunted road they had driven last summer in the ghostly half-twilight. Feeling the car move, watching the road get swallowed into it, Kath felt time collapse.

We've been here forever, she thought. *We are always driving this road, always going toward something that is always changing and is always the same. We are caught in a pattern and we cannot escape it because we are the pattern.* She looked over at Mick, so solid, so sure of himself, of his world, his eyes scanning the road, his hands so steady on the wheel. *He is in a different country,* she thought, *and there is no bridge.* She shivered.

Mick glanced at her. "You're cold," he said. "I told you not to wear short sleeves. The wind off the sea is chilling. And it'll be even colder come night. You'd better have my sweater."

He pulled off the road, braked, and shrugged the sweater off and passed it to her.

She slung it across her shoulders and tied the sleeves in front. "Thanks. That's better." She had a curious feeling of traveling back in time, of reliving her earlier experience. Or perhaps the two times were superimposed on one another, and she could not tell which was which.

A tang of wood smoke was in the air, and the little room was as crowded as it had been at the other gab. Folk had brought in extra benches and stools, and Kath saw that most of them were filled already, though she noted that unlike the other gab, no one this time was sitting on the table. Instead, it was laden with food. There were breads, salads, casseroles, and pies, while several bottles—at a guess, wine and whiskey both—stood sentinel at either end.

Quite a party, thought Kath. Trying to stay unnoticed, she and Mick chose chairs tucked into a corner beside the door. Smoke from the fireplace blew past in wisps.

Mick was speaking to her *sotto voce*, "This looks like a more formal occasion than the other gab. Tonight must be special."

Tiernon nodded agreement to Mick. "You have the right of it, boyo," he said. "To launch a local holiday. And there'll be a dance tomorrow, out on the headland. You were here at the Solstice last summer, weren't you? That was a time and a half. Things in such a jumble nobody knew what was the right way to go. You must have had a rare old time of it."

He turned to Kath as he spoke, but Mick intervened. "We certainly had an . . . interesting time," he said casually. "I wouldn't call it 'rare.' You'd know that better than I would. But what do you mean about the 'right way' to go? Did something go the wrong way?"

Tiernon gave him a sharp glance, then shrugged. "No, of course not, not really. Just a way of speaking. I did hear, though, that the young lady was taken ill." He looked at Kath again. "And that certainly wasn't supposed to happen."

Oh wasn't it?, thought Mick. *She was supposed to be taken somewhere, though, and you know all about that, don't you?* "Good of you to be concerned," he said. "But you can see, she's quite all right."

He took Kath's arm, but she pulled away and crossed to Elly in her chair by the fire. Two or three children were sitting at her feet, and she was bending to talk to them. At Kath's voice they looked at her, then squirmed closer to one another, creating space for her to join them.

"You'll enjoy this my dears," said Elly, looking blind-eyed straight at Kath. "It was Tiernon's favorite story when he was a little one. So small he could barely walk, and he'd scramble into my lap and ask for The Fisher-girl and the Selkie-man."

"Not so very long ago, there was a girl who took it into her head to go a-fishing. So, one summer, every afternoon the girl took a skiff and went out."

The string was pulling tight now, and Kath yielded to it.

Reeled in like a fish, she thought.

Mick saw it, and laid aside his own plate to keep an eye on her.

Elly did not pause, but the faintest lift in her voice told that she knew her audience.

"But she wasn't in luck's way, and she fished until sunset every day and nary a fish did she get. And at last she decided to give up. Well, everyone knows, it's on the last try that the magic happens. So as the sun went west and the air turned chill and little whitecaps sprang up all about her, she turned for shore with nothing to show for her day's work. But as she turned she said to herself,

'Show the thing I came to see,
or in the sun or in the sea.'

And wouldn't you know, right as she turned to pull in her line, there came a tug on the end of it.

'Oh-ho!' she thought to herself. 'Maybe I've snared a fish.' And she squared both oars and held the boat steady.

There came another tug, stronger than the first, and then a great surge and the sea heaved up like a hill and the boat rocked from side to side.

'What's this I've caught?,' she asked herself. 'By the feel it must be a porpoise or a baby whale.'

But whale or porpoise, it was like to capsize the boat with its thrashing about, so she grabbed the line in both fists and gave a heave! And as she heaved, up came a smooth brown head that shook drops of water in all directions, and she saw the shape of a seal in the water. Then two hands with webbed fingers took hold of the side of the boat and the boat began to rock and then to tip down and slide under the waves and she felt the webbed fingers take hold of her hand and pull her out of the boat and down and down and down they went past waving seaweed, past strange rocks and caverns, past wrecks of old ships with fishes swimming through the rigging, till they came to a golden sandy place with sea-flowers all around. Right through the middle they dived, and the sand spouted up like a fountain around them. Through a golden tunnel they swam, and came out—splash!—in a drowned castle.

She was in a candlelit hall with a fire burning in a wide hearth. And she saw that the seal-shape was gone, and in its place was a sea-prince dressed all in brown silk and his brown hair floating *out around his head like sea-grass, and he turned to the girl and said, 'The sea claims its own. Welcome to my kingdom.'*

And she said—"

"I'm coming."

Every head in the room turned, for the voice was not Elly's but Kath's, and she was rising to her feet, moving slowly, under water. Her eyes were unfocused, and her sudden pallor sent a jolt of alarm through Mick.

She walked unseeing into the table, knocking it off balance and herself with it. Mick reached out to intercept her as the table went over, and her fall dragged the tablecloth and a stack of dishes crashing after her.

Pandemonium followed, with people crowding close so that Mick had to shove them away to keep a space for her to breathe. A couple of men righted the table, and the women got busy clearing away broken plates.

Mick knelt beside Kath and saw the same sleepwalker's look on her face which he had seen at the Solstice party. But this time was different: more sudden, more abrupt. No one was expecting it, he could swear. The consternation around him was real, as was the genuine concern he saw in Greenie's face, and the deep compassion he read in Elly's blind gaze turned not toward Kath but to him. *How could she know?* he wondered.

Tiernon was squatting beside him. "Young lady took faint. Heat, most likely," he said easily. "It can get close in here, with all the people and the smoke. Get her outside in the fresh air."

Mick scooped her into his arms, headed out the door.

Tiernon followed, carrying a wooden bench. "Put her down here," he said. He settled the heavy bench out of the wind, and Mick lay Kath along it as gently as he could.

"I'll keep the crowd away," said Tiernon, and went back inside and shut the door.

Mick had Kath to himself. But he didn't have her at all. She was away, off somewhere where he couldn't follow.

This is getting to be a habit, he thought. *No, not a habit. A pattern. A repeating pattern. You asked for it. No, she asked for it. But you should have known,* he told himself. *You did know. You just didn't want to know you knew. And what happens now? Where has she gone? And how will I get her back?*

In the twilight of early stars he settled himself beside the bench, watching the pale, still face, listening to Kath's whispered breathing, almost in rhythm with the rush and hiss of waves running up the shingle below the house. The sound was hypnotic. He felt himself sliding into a half-trance when he saw that her eyes were open. "Kath. You all right?"

"Of course I'm all right. Why shouldn't I be?" She sat up and looked around. "What are we doing out here?"

"We're out here because you fainted, and I wanted to get you some air. Probably just the heat, the room was getting suffocating, but you scared me to death." He did not say *again*.

"I'm okay, really. Just . . ." She tried to stand up but he pushed her back.

"Just stay quiet for right now. I think you really are okay, but you ought to take it easy. I'm going to get you home. You stay here, and I'll do the goodbyes."

"No, I'll come with you. You don't have to treat me like an invalid."

Here we go, said Mick to himself.

She heard his thought and, quick to forestall him, said hurriedly, "Sorry. I didn't mean to snap. I'm just . . . surprised. I can't imagine why I fainted. I was feeling fine. Enjoying the story. And she had just got to the good part, hadn't she?"

The door opened, throwing a swatch of yellow lamplight against the dark. Greenie came out, all bustle and solicitation.

"How is she? Tiernon told us to give her some space. But we're all worried, and I just thought I'd have a wee look. Stay still, my dear, you shouldn't be up yet. Feeling better are you? You'll be thinking there's something in the air around here."

Kath tried to get a word in edgewise. "I'm fine. Really fine. I don't know what happened in there, but I—"

Mick cut in hastily.

"Yes, she's fine now. Nothing in the air, no of course not. A good night's sleep will make all the difference."

"Right you are. Can you get her up the path? It's a bit steep."

Kath sat up.

"I can walk by myself. I'm so sorry about this. Such a stupid way to behave. I don't make a habit of this, honestly. I'd better apologize to everyone." She swung her legs down from the bench.

"Not a bit of it," said Greenie. "No apology needed. But a cup of tea would be a good idea. Just to put you on the road. Won't be a minute." She disappeared into the house and was back in what seemed like seconds. "There now. Drink it while it's hot. This will get some strength into you."

Kath drank to please her, but the hot, sweet brew was reviving.

"There. That's a good girl. Drink it all. You'll be right as rain presently." Greenie patted her shoulder.

She downed it all, and color came back into her face.

"And now I think we'd better be getting back to our hotel," said Mick firmly. "Thanks for everything, Greenie. Say goodbye to Elly for us? And . . . uh, Tiernon? And explain that Kath's all right?"

"Of course, of course. Go along now. And drive safely. I'll explain to Elly and Tiernon—"

"Yes, well, I'm sure they'll understand." Mick grabbed Kath's arm, rushing escape from a conversation he emphatically didn't want to get started.

Kath let herself be led across the bridge and up the path, and she did not turn her head to look back as the foliage closed off sight of Elly's little house.

"Mick will you stop pulling my arm? I'm almost running as it is. I keep brushing into the tree branches."

He slowed down, but only a little.

"Sorry. I don't mean to rush you, but—"

"But you do mean to rush me. Talk about manners. Yours could use some mending. You all but told Greenie to shut up, you left her standing in the middle of a sentence, and it's her good manners, not yours, that kept things civil."

"Good manners be damned. Hers are not that great. She'll never stop talking, and I'm not about to stay and listen to her chatter all night. We need to get away and get home and get some peace and quiet. I've had it with selkies and sea-pigs and Grally Tuskers and mysteries and farewell rituals. A little sanity is what we need right now, a good dose of the ordinary. Come on."

Taking Leave

History does not always repeat itself, except, Mick noted wryly, *when it does.*

There was the car at the top of the path, right where he had left it. He bundled her in, but they were out of the woods and well on the road before he permitted himself a breath of relief.

"Okay. We're up and out. We've done what you wanted. We've made our courtesy call. And I don't mind saying I'm glad to see the last of that lot. They're a rum bunch for outsiders to deal with." He glanced over at her, inviting a response, not sure he'd get one.

She said slowly, "You know, I think you're right, Mick. I don't know if it's the place or the people or what, but when I'm here something strange takes over. Every time we come up here, I get all tangled up. I think I'm fine, and then weird things start happening, and I can't stop them. I feel like I am in the place where the stories are real, like I'm caught in something beyond my control. Or anybody's. I don't want to be Little Bridget any more. I want to get out of Elfland. I want to go home. Please."

"We'll go home. That's what I've been waiting to hear. Stories are just stories, you know. They don't have any power outside themselves. We can leave them behind. So here's what we'll do: we'll go back to the hotel, have dinner, get a good night's sleep and make an early start tomorrow. We'll be home in no time."

On the way back to the hotel, Kath fell asleep in the car. The night was cool, a fresh wind was blowing gently, and Mick thanked whatever lucky stars he had that they had got away without serious harm. *Goodbye Elverie*, he thought, grateful for passing traffic. *Back to the real world. And in the nick of time.* He glanced over at the sleeping Kath. She was restless, uneasy and half woke under his glance.

She twisted under the car coat. "Stop pulling. I'm falling too fast. The water is cold, and everything is green, rushing, rushing . . ." Her eyes closed and her voice trailed off. Suddenly she sat bolt upright and called out "Wait for me!" then fell back against the seat, eyes still closed. She did not speak again, but Mick could feel the apprehension building inside him, the knowledge, which had been gathering ever since the gab, of what he did not want to know.

After too long he pulled up in front of their hotel, deeply grateful for the sounds and smells of traffic, the noise and hustle of civilization, smog and dirt of a world defiantly other than the one they had left behind.

"Okay, we're here," he announced. "Time to wake up." He reached an arm to shake her gently. She came awake with reluctance, eyes unfocused and still full of dreams. Instinct told him to be matter of fact, practical.

"Come on, sleepyhead. Up we go. In half a tick you can be in a real bed with sheets and a pillow."

She was shivering, but not with the cold, though the air was chill. He nodded to the uniformed doorman, walked her through the doors, up in the lift door, got her down the carpeted hallway to their room, where she stood looking about her like an animal just emerging from a winter sleep. She was out on her feet and too tired to know it. The room tea-and-coffee pot was on the night-stand, two mugs next to it.

"I'll make some tea," he said.

"No, don't!"

"What's the matter?"

She was staring with horror at the tea-things, pointing at a mug.

"It's only a tea-mug, love. It's not going to eat you."

"Yes, it is." Her eyes were huge, dark with fear. "That's just what it's going to do."

"Letting your imagination run a bit wild, aren't you?"

"It's got a crack in it, right the way from one side to the other. It's the same crack as at the Solstice. The one I fell through. Mick, I'm scared." Her voice was tense, her throat constricted.

"You're letting your imagination run away with you."

At that she exploded. "Will you please stop saying that! Nothing is running away with me."

"Okay. I'm sorry. But will you please, for me, not let this take you over? A crack is just a crack; it's not the hand of fate. Let's forget the tea. You're so tired you don't even know it. What you need is some down time without a head full of stories that jerk you around. Bed for you, lady, and pronto. Come on."

She complied without protest, let him help her undress, pull a nightgown over her head and tuck her into bed and draw the curtains. Her trust in him broke his heart. She relaxed almost immediately, and turned on her side with a little sigh, but he waited until her regular breathing told him she was asleep. Only then, settled in the armchair did he unleash the fear he had been holding back. Since the Solstice celebration he had been suppressing his anxiety, denying his worry as overreaction. *You don't want to think the one you love may be crazy.* The minute he said it, even in his head, he flinched as if he had stepped on a thorn. *No. Yes.* Something was very wrong. He didn't know what, but whatever it was, it could no longer be dismissed. It was serious, and it scared him as much as it scared Kath. She was falling through the crack in the teacup, between the slats of the troll-bridge, pulled down and down into the water sliding past. There was that about Kath that eluded him, always had, probably always would. She would always be ahead of him, running toward the unknown, toward the rushy glen.

What he did know was that although he could not live without her, he had never truly lived with her, and that he was coming close to losing her. How glibly in his journal article he had written about Elly: "*What she spoke we saw.*" He cringed now at the words on the page, at the cliché, the figure of speech, the bullshit. Kath's words, straight from the heart, came back to him from that first night at the gab: "*I was there. In the story.*" *She wasn't kidding.* His own words from last night came back to haunt him. "*Stories are just stories, you know. We can leave them behind.*" *Wrong, wrong, wrong.* He forced himself to face the truth that his analytical mind, his education, even his chosen profession, had all concealed from him the unwelcome truth that he didn't know what he was talking about, and Kath did. The truth about story-telling, the real truth that Kath and Lame Elly and Tiernon knew, that everybody knew but Mick the Folklorist, Mick the Collector, Mick the Motif-tabulator, was that stories had power in their own right, power to re-make the world word by word, again and again, a new creation with each new telling. And each new world came out of the partnership between the teller and the listener. It was collaboration, not entertainment.

But what came next? He didn't know and there was no one who could tell him. Kath was sleeping soundly, her breath deep and even. It wasn't 10 p.m. yet. He had to clear the cobwebs out of his head. He closed the door to the room as quietly as he could, and set out to walk off his anxiety.

The Click of the Latch

The minute Kath heard the door latch click into
place behind Mick, she sat up and threw back
the covers. There was, she knew, no time to lose.
She slid into a pair of jeans, pulled on a cotton
shirt and a cardigan over it, wiggled her feet
into clogs. She felt breathless, like the start of
holidays when she was a child. Everything
waiting, everything still to come. She retrieved
her purse from the chair by the bed. *How much
money? Some bills. Enough to get her there and a bit
over*. She realized she was running a race, and
consciously, deliberately slowed her pace. *Calm
down*, she told herself. *More haste, less speed. Who
said that? Somebody in a book*. But when she

retrieved the memory, she realized it was not a very good one. *But I can't just leave. I have to say goodbye.*

There was a pad of scratch paper on the dresser. What to write? Too abrupt and he'd be hurt. And she didn't want to hurt him, dear Mick. Too tender and he'd be after her like a shot. She didn't want that either. The note she finally scribbled would have to do.

She folded the paper, wrote his name on the outside, and propped it where she knew he would see it. Then she slung her bag over her shoulder, left the light burning for Mick, and went forth. The latch clicked with finality behind her as she hurried out the door in search of transport.

By curious coincidence a taxi was just pulling up at the corner, the passenger already getting out and turning to pay. He disappeared into the foot traffic, and Kath hurried to catch the taxi before she lost this chance.

Please Please Please

With no idea where he was going, Mick let his feet carry him while his mind revolved the problem. He was grateful that the streets were unfamiliar, the people indifferent, the isolation of a stranger in a strange town throwing him back on his own resources. *Well, then, use them; think it through.* The process was wrenching, and took him the better part of an hour. It came down to this: standing by or resisting while Kath struggled with and against the forces pulling her was no good for either of them — frustrating for him; maddening for her. To really help her, he'd have to alter course, go with her, however much that went against the grain. This conclusion finally arrived at, he was suddenly eager to tell her. He swung on his heel and started back.

Unlocking the door, he called out "Kath? I've been thinking . . ." before realizing that the room was empty. Maybe she was in the bathroom? He called again, knocked. "Kath? I've . . . Kath?"

No answer.

Then he saw the note propped against the stack of books, his name scrawled in Kath's familiar handwriting. Slowly, deliberately he sat down at the desk and unfolded the paper, knocking over the books in the process. One landed on the floor, flopping open at a much-thumbed page. He paid no heed, but began to read the lines scrawled across the page.

Mick dear —

Please understand. I have to do this.

I'll be all right, I promise.

Please give me time and don't come looking.

Please please please understand.

I know what I have to do.

Mick, I do love you.

Kath

His first reaction was no reaction at all, just numbness, a blank spot on the surface of time. He held the paper in his hand, staring at the few lines. *"Please please please."* How long he sat looking he didn't know, but what difference did it make? It wasn't going to change anything. So where had she gone? *Stupid question.* There was only one place she would go. Did she expect him to follow, though she'd told him not to? In ordinary circumstances he'd have gone after her straightaway, but these weren't ordinary circumstances. He wanted to find her, bring her back, but when he considered the state he suspected she was in, he realized that pursuing her might tip her over the edge, cause her to explode as on that night in the restaurant.

How long had she been gone? She must have been waiting for him to leave. Putting up with him. Letting him tuck her into bed. And all the while . . . All the fine insights of his walk drained away, and he felt himself beginning to be angry. *Hell of a thing to do. You'd think she didn't trust me.* The anger felt good, and he let it build. *All right. Forget about it. If she's on her way, she's on her way.*

But he realized he was unconsciously listening for the sound of the door opening.

Every sound from outside, every street noise translated itself into Kath's returning footsteps. Her key in the lock, her quick, light step. Telling himself to forget was futile. He couldn't.

He bent to pick up the book he had knocked on the floor. It was *The Welsh Fairy Book*, its fluttered pages fallen open to the picture of the knight with his arms out and the water-fay combing her hair. The fall had knocked the cover loose and it looked like the last gathering of leaves was pulled loose from the spine. *Have to mend that*, he told himself absently. He sat at the desk, the book with its picture in front of him, and memories came in an avalanche. *Yesterday in town, the book prowl, sharing treasures. Before the gab. Was that the last time we were happy?*

Loss overwhelmed him.

He re-read the note, folded it and used it to mark the place where the book had fallen open. He heard his own voice telling Kath, "*You're too flighty for my comfort, and you could take wing at any minute. I need to have you firmly tethered to your perch.*"

Well, she had escaped the tether, flown from the perch, run away from the story.

He remembered the Solstice and Tiernon saying, *"You must fight for her"* and Greenie telling him about the two brothers.

Thanks for the advice, Greenie. I wish I could take it. I'd fight for Kath, if she'd let me. Greenie, I'd fight you for Kath, I'd fight Elly for Kath, I'd fight the bloody whole lot of you for Kath. But I can't fight Kath for Kath. She is the last enemy and the strongest.

"We're not enemies," said Kath in his head, *"and it's not a fight. It's just the way things are. I didn't ask for this, but I must see it through."*

"Through to what?" he asked her.

"To where I know what's going on. Where I know who I am and how I fit into this whole crazy thing. And you have to let me do that."

"Let you?" The irony made him wince. *"How can I stop you? How do I even know what to stop you from? You're following some will 'o the wisp that I can't see. Even if I went after you and brought you back — again — I couldn't keep you tethered. Not against your will. I've tried every which way I know, and you still keep going back and going back. But if you do find out what's going on, I hope you'll let me in on the secret. Because I've got news for you, lady. Whatever's happening to you, it's happening to me too."*

How long the silent argument went on he could never afterward remember, but he finally gave it up in disgust. *This is silly*, he thought. *This is not Kath. If there's one thing you've learned, it's that you don't know what Kath will say or think, don't know at any moment what she will do. So stop pretending. Let it go. Forget it.* As the words spun round and round, he realized all at once that he was dead tired, stretched himself out on the rumpled bed and fell at once into exhausted sleep, the words still spinning in his head.

Something the Cat Dragged In

Standing on a low stool, Greenie was dusting the bottles behind the bar, humming to herself, relishing the quiet. Though she liked it when the place was full with the noise of people eating and drinking, she also enjoyed having it to herself while doing the simple chores of polishing, cleaning, setting things in order, preparing for the daily onslaught. The slightly musty smell of beer, the sharp, astringency of glass cleaner, the oily scent of wood polish, all were part of her enjoyment. The oblique light of the just-risen sun gave the room a greenish cast of under water, a room full of shifting shadows, and beyond it the dark hallway slanting to the half-glass front door. Giving a final flick of the duster, she was about to step down when a flutter caught her eye. Something outside the front door was moving. In the aqueous light it looked like seaweed under a wave. She looked closer. It was a hand waving. At the same time the doorknob rattled.

Setting down her bottle of spray, Greenie wiped her hands on her apron and walked down the passage to see with no surprise that the face belonging to the waving hand was Kath's. The doorknob continued to rattle frantically.

She swung the door wide, and Kath almost fell into the room.

"Well look at you! Goodness sakes!"

"I was afraid you wouldn't hear me."

"I'd have heard you at the land's end, the racket you were making. It's only a doorknob; no need to kill it."

"Sorry."

She didn't look sorry. She looked disheveled, distraught, disarranged. She was shaking.

"Sit down," said Greenie. "I'll put on some coffee."

She disappeared into the kitchen, but was back in a short time with a tray, a pot, and two mugs. She poured the coffee, dark and steaming. "Black, right? I remember. Drink up."

Kath took a long swallow, set her mug down, took a deep breath, started to speak, stopped.

"I thought you'd gone home. Are you by yourself? Where's Mick?"

"He didn't come."

"I can see that. But he'll come later?"

"No. At least, I don't think so. But I don't know. I'm no good for him until I get my head settled, and he's better off without me."

There's two ways of thinking about that, thought Greenie, but she bit back the remark. No sense meddling at this stage. There was enough going on without interference.

"How did you get here?"

"Took a taxi from the hotel last night. But it was still dark when I got here, so I've been waiting outside until I thought somebody'd be up. Pretty chilly." She shivered and rubbed her arms. "I knew you wouldn't be open yet," Kath continued, "but I figured if I hung around long enough, somebody would be about. When I saw you through the door, I guess I just lost it, afraid you wouldn't see me or would think I was a tradesman or something."

"A tradesman? At this hour? Better if you'd called ahead, though. It's the jump of the season. How long are you here for? We're filling up, but I've still got that little room. I don't usually let it unless we're overfull. The one you and Mick . . ." She hesitated, wary, fearing to say too much or too little, aware of knowing more than Kath knew about why she was here, what had drawn her back. This was a tricky time, the balance delicate, the outcome far from certain.

"The room Mick and I had at the Solstice. It's okay to say it. I was thinking of that room, hoping it was free."

"Yes, it's free, but it's not much of a room, as you know. Still, it's a place to lay your head. Where's your luggage?"

"Haven't got any luggage." Kath laughed, but awkwardly, embarrassed to have been so impulsive. "I just . . . walked out. Didn't bring anything but the clothes I'm standing in. Not even a toothbrush."

"You look like something the cat dragged in. No way to pass the time, standing around in the dark. Some hot food will warm you up. I'll share it. I'm hungry enough for two."

Greenie disappeared into the kitchen, leaving Kath at the little table. She was here. Without knowing why, without completely understanding how she had managed it, acting under a compulsion she didn't understand, she was here. She was drained physically and emotionally, at the end of her tether. But she was here.

So high was her level of nervous tension that she hadn't known it. But now it escaped like air out of a balloon, leaving her limp and directionless. What would happen next she had no idea. She wasn't sure what she wanted. She didn't even know what questions to ask. She'd done all she knew how to do and somebody else would have to take it from there. She was too tired to sleep, but slid into a timeless limbo where all that had passed was a fast-fading dream. She tried to hold on to it, but it disappeared like mist. She had been here forever and would go on equally forever.

Greenie re-emerged from the kitchen carrying a large tray laden with eggs, toast, fried ham, a pot of wild berry jam. She set the tray down with a thump that brought Kath back from forever to now. "There you are," said Greenie. "Put yourself outside of that, and maybe you'll get some color in your cheeks. Thin as a rail you are." She gave Kath a narrow glance. "What you been doing with yourself?"

"Oh, Greenie . . ." Kath turned her hands palm up in a helpless gesture. "I haven't been doing anything, really, except . . . wondering. Ever since Mick and I were here at the Solstice last year, everything has been so strange. I have strange dreams. At least I think they're dreams, but it's hard to tell. And then we came back, and I thought that would help, but it only made things worse. Because . . . Tiernon. I needed to see him."

She waited for some comment from Greenie that would tell her how to proceed. But none was forthcoming, so she stumbled on.

"If that sounds confused, it's because I am. I'm a mess."

Greenie's earthy practicality came to the rescue. "Well, you certainly are a mess, that's for sure, but wouldn't anybody be after standing about in the cold all night? It's a wonder you can string two words together, never mind make sense. And not even a change of clothes. You could use a bath and some clean duds, if you want my opinion. But we'll see to all that. Now, eat up. And don't think about anything for a while but putting food in your mouth."

Easy enough to do. The food was hot and good-tasting and plentiful, the eggs softly scrambled and creamy with just enough pepper for fragrance, the toast crisp and buttered, the ham salt and tangy. The tea was almost scalding, but sweet and with a smoky flavor that lingered on the back of her tongue. Kath tucked in. There were second helpings. She ate steadily for half an hour, pushing back her plate finally with a sigh not just of contentment, but relief. Greenie was right: the hot food warmed her and brought her back to herself. On a full stomach Kath felt more like a person and less like the walking dead.

A hot bath was next. Greenie supplied soap and a towel and Kath lost no time in shrugging out of her sweater and travel-grubby, rumpled, shirt and jeans, peeling off bra and pants, and kicking off her shoes. She ran the tub full, added a generous splash of bath oil and lowered her exhausted, grimy self into the steaming water, where she lay soaking until she almost fell asleep. But the water began to cool, sure sign that it was time to scrub, climb out, wrap herself in the towel and head for bed.

She closed the bedroom door and leaned against the solid wood, a barricade between her and what she wasn't ready to deal with. The little room was just as she remembered: the slanted ceiling under the steeply pitched roof, the worn boards of the bare floor, the dormer window at the foot of the bed with a view over the tree-tops to the thin silver horizon of the sea. In her nostrils was the smell of dust and shadows and the fragrance of old wood. She recalled the curious feeling the room had given her, that it was a passageway between worlds. She opened the window, breathing the fresh, early morning, the faint tang of salt from the wind off the sea. The light was clear and sharp, sun just lighting the treetops.

The room welcomed her. The bed took up most of the space, and looked so inviting she dropped the towel and slid gratefully between the cool, fresh sheets, feeling their crisp caress on her clean, naked skin. Almost at once she felt her body relax; the muscles she had for so long held under tight control now allowed to loosen and go slack. Her eyelids came down of their own accord, shutting away the outside world. Sleep covered her like a blanket.

✦   ✦   ✦

"Wicken Tree Inn, good morning. This is Greenie. Can I help you?"

"Is . . . I mean, good morning. Greenie, it's Mick. Is—"

"Thought it might be you. Where are you?"

"I'm still in town. At the hotel. Is she—"

"Yes, she's here. She's all right, Mick, just worn out. I've fed her and put her to bed. Will I have her call you when she wakes?"

"Only if she wants to. But will you give her a message for me?" He made her repeat it twice to make sure she got it right, then hung up.

✦   ✦   ✦

Kath was looking out the window, over the tops of the trees to the sea. The wind was blowing hard and steady off the sea, and she leaned on the window-sill and felt it blow her hair. The air was clear and bright, and there were no shadows. Tiernon came walking toward her over the horizon. In the water under his feet fish were leaping. She reached out to touch him, but he shook his head.

She said, *"Where are you? Where am I?"*

He said, *"We are in the same place when you have the sight to see. I am walking over a grassy plain filled with flowers."* He gestured to the leaping fish. *"Do you see my lambs where they are playing in the meadow? This is the world you came to find. This is the world that calls you. Do you see where you are?"* said Tiernon. *"You are sailing above the tree tops, skimming over the wood in a little boat. It is the boat of the girl in the story. You are the girl in the story."*

She said *"That is Elly's story."*

He said *"It is all one story."*

As he spoke, Kath felt the little boat tilt dangerously, and looked down to see the webbed brown paws of the selkie clutching the gunwale. One of the paws reached up, wet and dripping from the sea, and she felt the webbed fingers take hold of her hand and pull her out of the boat and down . . .

"No!" she cried out, and fell wide awake into the little room.

It was so real. The panic as she went under, the water closing green and cold over her head. She sat quite still and gradually her breathing slowed. She looked about her. It was broad daylight, afternoon sun streaming in the window. Not waves tossed around her but sheets and coverlet: she was safe and dry in bed; the sea was far away. No webbed paw was pulling her hand. No selkie was there. No one was there at all. She was weak with relief and the knowledge that she had been dreaming. She lay back down, snuggled her head into the pillow for comfort, pulled the covers over her head for safety.

But she could not fall asleep no matter how she tried. She turned uneasily, shifting her legs in vain effort to get comfortable. Her eyes ached with fatigue, but when she closed them the bright sunlight burned through, and they popped open of themselves. It was no use. She knew she was awake, so she might as well get up. As she threw back the covers, she saw the knob on the door turn very slowly. Something was standing there. Something was coming for her. She stood mute; she couldn't breathe, she couldn't scream. In a moment the door would swing open and there would be the nameless, indescribable thing she had been dreading all her life. It was here, it would be now.

"Who are you?," she whispered. "What do you want from me?" She tried to run but she was still in bed and her legs were tangled in the bedclothes that washed over her like waves and weighed her down. She struggled to get free and escape, but each move was feeble, her muscles had no strength, the sheets held her back, and the room stretched to an endless treadmill where she ran in slow motion without advancing.

The door swung open, and she blinked and her eyes dazzled as she saw a silhouette framed the open doorway. The dream was real. The boat was tilting. A jolt of terror went through her.

"Awake at last are you?" said Greenie. She bustled into the little room, filling it with her energy.

"I looked in once or twice, but you were dead to the world. And now . . . my goodness but these sheets are a tangle. Looks like you've been riding the night mare. And me thinking all this time you were getting a nice rest. I did a wash-and-dry of tablecloths and napkins, so I threw in your clothes. No trouble, and you'll have something clean to put on."

She draped shirt, jeans, bra and pants over the bottom of the bed, hung the cardigan on the bedpost, talking nonstop all the while.

"It's getting on for evening. You've slept the day away. Come downstairs when you're ready. There's someone here wants to see you." She moved toward the doorway, hesitated, turned. "Before I forget it, your Mick called a little while ago. Did you tell him where you were going? Or did he guess? Doesn't matter. He gave me a message for you. Made me say it twice to be sure I got the words right. Said to tell you 'don't spook the horses.' I hope you know what that means, for I certainly don't."

"I know what that means," said Kath. She sat up and reached for the clothes at the bottom of the bed.

Reflections

Kath hesitated in the doorway. The big television over the bar was turned off, making the blacked-out screen a mirror that gave back the room at a tilt so that she felt like a spectator looking down from a balcony seat. It created an odd sensation, like being in two rooms at once: one real, the other a reflection. Greenie was sitting at a table talking with Tiernon. As if she felt Kath's glance, she looked up and their eyes met in the darkened screen.

"There you are," said Greenie. "We were just talking about you."

I'll bet you were, thought Kath. *The crazy lady who keeps coming back, the nut-case who passes out and knocks over the furniture. Why do you suppose she's here?* "Oh? And did you have a lot to say?"

"We weren't gossiping," said Tiernon before Greenie could answer, ignoring the patent hostility in Kath's voice. "I didn't know you were here until Greenie told me. But when she did I wanted to see you, see how you were. We were all worried about you after the gab."

"I'm fine," said Kath, sliding carefully into a chair so as not to knock it over.

"Better than you were, that's for certain," said Greenie. "You look a bit more like a real person and a bit less like a store-window dummy—all bones and plaster. Tiernon here, he had an idea, if you were feeling up to it. That's what we were taking about."

Ashamed of her show of temper, Kath belatedly remembered to mind her manners. "I'm sorry if I sounded rude. I didn't mean to. But I just woke up, and I'm still a bit foggy." She turned to Tiernon. "What's your idea?"

"There's a local celebration out on the headland," Tiernon told her, "I was telling your friend about it last night. It's a contest between winter and spring. A festival with flowers and singing and they choose a girl to act out the Story, to be the ... to be the Bride."

If she noticed the hesitation Kath chose to ignore it. *I've already been a bride*, she thought to herself. *Once is enough.* And to Greenie, "What Bride? Whom does she marry?"

"Well, it depends on the Story," Greenie explained. "Sometimes there's the Contest to see who wins her. Sometimes she just stands there and gets pelted with flowers. Sometimes she has a bigger part to play. But it has to be somebody new. To buy Spring, from Winter you see, pay the price for the new season. Tiernon here thought you might be just the right person."

Oh no you don't, thought Kath. *I'm not getting roped in again, like at the Solstice. No more mumbo jumbo for me, thank you very much.* Aloud, she said, "But why me? I'm not just new, I'm temporary. A bird of passage. Don't you want somebody who'll be around? To usher spring into summer and all that?"

"No, no. You'll be fine. It wants someone fresh."

Privately Kath wondered what Greenie meant by "fresh" but decided she had been rude enough. "Well, if it's all right with everybody. I don't want to be an intruder."

Greenie laughed, a big, comfortable chuckle. "Bless you, you won't be intruding. You just have to fit the qualifications."

"And what are those?"

"Be young. Be ready. Be willing."

"That doesn't sound like much."

"It's enough. You'll soon get the hang of it. And everybody wants to help. It carries good luck, you see, to be part of bringing in the season."

The words of her dream came back to her.

This is the world you came to find. This is the world that calls you. You are sailing above the treetops, skimming over the wood in a little boat. It is the boat in the story. You are the girl in the story.

Oh no, said a voice in her head. I am not the girl in the story. I won't be her.

She stopped, embarrassed, but the others hadn't heard her thoughts. She fell back on an old dodge.

"But if it's a party, a celebration, I won't look right in these jeans and a shirt. I don't have anything else to wear." Privately she laughed at her own words. *I sound like a teenager getting ready for a dance*, she thought.

"We can fix you up," said Greenie. "There's trunks of old clothes up in the attic. You're a bit skinny, but we'll find something and make it fit. Come up with me and we'll have a look. You stay here, Tiernon, and we'll surprise you."

The attic, high up under the rooftree, was adjacent to her bedroom, reached by a low door she hadn't noticed before. Entering it, she had again the sensation of moving between two worlds. She ducked her head to enter a dusty, shadowy space stacked with boxes and trunks, an old bedstead dismantled and propped against a wall, a full-length mirror with tarnished silvered glass whose tilted reflection gave everything the green and slanted underwater look of the common room.

Greenie pulled out a trunk, leather-bound and humpbacked. Throwing back the lid, she began shaking out the contents, draping them over the bedstead.

"Here's something might do. Try it on."

Once a deep green but faded from many washings, the dress might have once been somebody's go-to-meeting finery that had seen better days. It was long-sleeved, tight at the waist, with buttons up the back, falling softly around her ankles. It fitted Kath as if made for her, and brought out the green of her eyes. but was clearly from another era.

From another era, thought Kath, *or another world.*

"And this flowered apron to go with? Here, I'll tie it for you." Greenie stepped back, satisfied. "Makes you look like an apple tree in bloom. And look—here in the corner of the trunk—a wreath. Just the thing. Probably from an old hat. A bit squashed from being in the trunk. Never mind. They'll have lots of real wreaths tomorrow."

"Now! Look at yourself in the mirror."

Obediently, Kath looked at her reflection, but so streaked and tarnished was the mirror, and so dusty was its surface that not herself but a dim, green and grey ghost looked back at her through a silver mist. She was a revenant from another time, another story. Behind her reflection the mirror shifted and rippled like waves on a cloudy day. She shivered as if she had walked over her own grave.

"You'll do fine," said Greenie.

As Kath opened her mouth to protest, Elly's words from the Fisher-Girl story came back to her:

Everyone knows it's on the last try that the magic happens.

From a great distance, Kath heard herself ask *"What must I do?"*
"You'll know," said Elly.
"All right, then, I'll do it."

Now ... What?

With a scrunch of tires on gravel, Mick swung into the car park and braked to a stop. In one continuous motion he switched off the engine, got out, slammed the door, and started running. He covered the distance to the inn at full speed, but once in the hall he stopped short. The cool darkness of the hall was like a cave, and the hands of the clock stood at ten. Beyond, in the common room, he could hear voices. Driving up had been an agony of suspense and terror, and now that he was here . . . what? His eyes were gritty, he was rumpled and dirty and unshaven, and he had no plan, no idea of what he might meet, or what he could or should do next.

He found himself in the doorway, looking across the room at a table by the bar where sat a man and a woman. The woman was Greenie, as he would have expected, but the man, half-turned away, was a cipher. Conversation died as Greenie looked up and saw him. No one spoke, and he felt awkward at the silence, an uninvited guest at a gathering.

"Well here's another cat fallen in the fishpond. What you been doing, Mick, to get so scruffy-looking? Never mind, doesn't matter. It's good to see you."

That was Greenie, a welcome with a sting in it. Or a sting with a welcome behind it. Mick wasn't sure which. *But that*, he thought ruefully, *is a good description of my state of mind for the past months: never sure what is going on; never sure what the message is.*

"Where's Kath? What have you done with her?" Even to him his voice sounded harsh, ill-prepared for speech.

The man, Mick recognized him now as Tiernon, pulled out a chair and gestured him to sit. "I guess you mean your young lady?"

"Sorry," said Mick. "I don't mean to sound boorish. But I'm worried about her."

319

Tiernon nodded. "Yes, she seems a bit high-strung. Very intense. You can be easy, boyo. We have done nothing with her or to her."

"Then where is she?"

"Out on the headland with the Revelers. You can go there if you want, and see for yourself, but maybe you'll want a wash and brush-up first? And a bite to eat?"

He seemed so ordinary, so matter-of-fact, that Mick's belligerence was disarmed. "What Revelers?" he asked, more to gain time than to get information.

"It's the Spring Festival," said Tiernon. "We keep the old customs up here, as you've no doubt noticed. Contest between Winter and Spring. Spring wins Summer from Winter. Pays the high price. Revelers act the Story. We've invited your girl to take part."

"What kind of part?" asked Mick. "If it's acted out, how will she know what to do?"

"She has only to follow along and everything will sort itself out," said Tiernon. "Everybody knows the Story. But it's a longish ceremony. Goes on for most of the day. You have plenty of time yet. Let Greenie get you some coffee and a bite, and we'll go out to the headland together."

320

"I wouldn't say 'no' to breakfast," said Mick, realizing as he said the words how hungry he was. "This is getting to be a habit, you always giving me breakfast, Greenie."

"That's because you keep turning up at mealtimes," said Greenie. "Any road, it's my job. This is an inn, after all. I'll see what I can find in the kitchen."

She disappeared through the swing-door, leaving Mick and Tiernon wondering what to say to each other. At least Mick was wondering. Tiernon seemed content to sit without conversation, which left a vacancy Mick felt uncomfortably required to fill.

"Ah . . . tell me more about this Story. A local tale is it? Or a ritual and some standard characters?"

"We take it seriously," said Tiernon.

"My apologies," said Mick carefully. "I'm a bit groggy from driving all night, and I used the wrong words. Of course you take it seriously. I was just wondering how Kath would fit in. I had the impression that such rituals were for the in-group."

"Your young lady takes it seriously, I'd say. Seems right in sympathy with what's going on. I remember her from the Solstice, though she did get a bit carried away."

"Not this time. That's what I'm here to prevent, if I can."

"Ah," said Tiernon, "if you can. But prevention's a risky business. You don't know what you might be stirring up. I wouldn't interfere, if I were you."

"But you're not me," said Mick. "And I'm not you. We're different."

"Not so different as you might think," said Tiernon.

"I think Kath can tell the difference," said Mick.

"Challenging me, are you, boyo?" said Tiernon.

"No," said Mick. "Just continuing the conversation."

Tiernon said nothing in reply, and the conversation lapsed into silence.

The Dance

It was midday now, the overhead sun appearing and disappearing in an inconstant, clouds-and-sunshine sky, and Kath had been dancing with the sun for hours. Or days. Or years. She didn't know and didn't care. Time stood still or revolved endlessly upon itself. She was dizzy with the dance and the endless turning, drunk with laughter and joy and the sunlight off the sea and the wind from the west and the lilting song of the pan-pipe and the high clear music of singing voices. She was a part of the dance and always had been and always would be, and that was enough. Whatever impulse had driven her to this place like a homing bird was at peace now that she was here. She led the dancers, their arms linked around each other's waists, moving in a curving line that bent and twisted and turned in and around itself but always sunwise following the right-hand path, a labyrinthine pattern that spiraled in and in, and she was at the center. She saw Elly take off her shawl and wave it high above her head, and at that signal saw all the other dancers swing away from her, forming a half-circle around her against the straight line of the cliff.

What now? She faced the dancers hesitantly, uncertain of her part. They were taking off their garlands, pulling them apart and pelting her with the flowers, a soft, scented barrage that drove her backward step by step. She tried to catch the flowers, but they came too quick. Then they stopped, and the laughter and the singing stopped and everything fell silent. There was a hush, a breath, a sense of expectation. A last missile, a full branch of apple blossoms arced through the air and grazed her the temple. Half dodging, she put up her hand and caught it. It felt strangely light in her hand. *Like a feather*, she thought. But the feather was pulling her, tugging at her hand to make her turn toward the cliff-edge.

✦ ✦ ✦

The wind was blowing hard and steady off the sea, and she leaned on the window-sill and felt it blow her hair. The air was clear and bright, and there were no shadows. Tiernon waved to her from the fishing-boat, and she waved back.

She said, "Where are we?"

He said, "In the world you came to find."

She felt the little boat tilt dangerously, and looked down, down over the edge to the sea below the cliffs and the waves crashing against the rocks. The beast was there. The webbed brown paws of the selkie clutched the side of the boat. One of the paws reached up, wet and dripping from the sea . . . and she felt the webbed fingers take hold of her hand and pull her into the center of the maze, the heart of everything.

✦ ✦ ✦

As he walked out onto the headland with Tiernon, Mick had felt both relieved and exasperated. Whatever he had feared for Kath, whatever nightmare visions had run through his head on that endless drive, what he now saw seemed harmless enough: a country dance, a spring celebration with flower garlands, men and women and boys and girls all in a ring, passing and re-passing in an endless dance. The grass where they danced was trampled and scuffed to bare earth by their feet. Somebody — he couldn't see who — was playing a pan-pipe, an archaic tune with rising and falling notes and odd intervals like the song of a bird.

"Looks like they've been dancing for quite a while," he remarked to Tiernon.

"Since sunrise," said Tiernon, and his voice rang so strangely that Mick looked at him in sudden surprise. He looked bigger, shoulders broader and arms longer than Mick remembered.

He could see Kath, dipping and turning in a double ring pattern with a hand to each dancer as they passed, her lovely face tranced and joyful. The scene seemed wholly innocent, and Kath was simply a part of it. She had a garland of flowers on her head, and she was wearing a long skirt and apron. The skirt, flowered pink on green like apple blossoms, swirled and flared as she turned, dancing with her like flowering trees in a spring breeze. She looked like springtime personified.

What did you expect? Mick chided himself, *a ritual sacrifice with Kath as the goat led to the slaughter? You're letting her imagination run away with you. Besides, you only have to look at her to see that she's in her element.* Mick noticed, almost as an afterthought, that the dancers were winding and circling closer and closer to the cliffs. *But it's their turf,* he told himself. *They must know what they're doing.* Then at an unseen signal the dancers swung away from Kath and formed a half-circle around her. She stood facing them, her back to the cliffs, laughing, uncertain, not knowing what to expect. An alarm rang in Mick's head: *you'd walk right off the edge of the world and not even know it. She wouldn't,* his thought told him. *They wouldn't.*

And before he could even realize his fear, the mock-attack began, each dancer pulling apart a garland to throw the flowers at Kath. At first she tried to catch them, but they came too fast and she retreated under the barrage, but they began to pile up around her so that she stood ankle-deep in flowers, balancing unsteadily just steps from the edge of the cliff.

Someone thrust a flowering branch into Mick's hand. "Here. Join the fun."

The branch was in full bloom, laden with blossoms, and it weighed curiously heavy in his hand. *Like a club,* he thought, but still he raised his arm and threw, and as he threw he called her name — "Kath!" — and she turned and saw him and then everything happened at once and in slow motion. The branch arced end over end across the air and Mick saw it strike her on the temple.

He hadn't meant to throw hard.

"It's only flowers," said Tiernon.

And it was only flowers. A flower could hardly be lethal.

He saw her reach her hand and turn, entranced, to look beyond the cliff to the sea, to someone there.

He heard again the voice of the sea-prince in Elly's story: *"The sea claims its own."*

"What do you think you're doing?" he asked, running toward her. "Kath," he said. "Kath, look out. You're too close . . . Kath! No!" shouted Mick. "Get away from that! You're right on the edge. You'll fall if you don't watch out." Breaking free of the hands that tried to stop him, he ran toward her.

She balanced uncertainly, drawn hypnotically to the dream-confused images that filled her vision. The depths were pulling her.

✦ ✦ ✦

"I'd look down through the cracks at the water sliding and past underneath. I was scared to death, because I felt like the current of the river was pulling me down and down." It was Mick, and he was so close to the truth, and yet he didn't understand.

"No, not exactly. I'm not afraid of falling, Mick. I'm afraid of wanting to fall."

✦ ✦ ✦

Reaching out, wanting to fall, leaning voluptuously into her desire and fear, she stepped forward, out over thin air, broke the tether that held her to earth and gave herself to the ecstasy of free fall, only to be pulled up short with a violent jerk as at the last moment something stopped her short. Tethered yet free, she dangled perilously between land and sea, a puppet swinging awkwardly in midair while the waves surged and crashed below her.

Afterward, Mick could never remember clearly how it happened. He saw Kath reach out to an unseen hand and start to walk off the edge of the world. He made an impossible lunge and grabbed with both hands as she fell but felt her slipping from his grasp. Her fall dragged him flat and half over the cliff, holding on for dear life to handfuls of skirt from which Kath dangled precariously, only a few feet of faded cotton between her and the waiting sea. For a moment he lay still, all his being concentrated in his hands and arms. Then, like a whisper, he felt the thin fabric that held her begin to tear under her weight. He felt her sag perceptibly. Slowly, agonizingly, his muscles cracking with the strain and the flimsy cloth ripping further with every pull, Mick hauled at her weight. As she came up he dragged her body over the edge. He could feel his shoulder crack and then a searing pain as his arm popped out of its socket and he lay Kath safe on dry land, where she collapsed, sick and dizzy and grateful to be alive.

No one spoke. The wind siffled over the grass. Mick and Kath lay breathing, the only two people on the planet.

It was Greenie's voice, flat and practical, that cut sharply across the moment and broke

330

the spell that held them. She turned to the dancers. "It's time for you all to go home now. The Dance is over. The Story is done with, finished for this year." And then to Mick, "You need somebody to tend to that shoulder."

As the dancers dispersed, walking away over the grass in little groups of twos and threes, Tiernon looked down at Mick. "Are you in pain?"

"It hurts, yes. But I can stand it."

"No need to be tough. Better let me have a look at it." He bent to Mick, took the hand that lay, awkward and limp on the grass as if it did not belong to the body it grew from, and before Mick could protest gave it a sudden powerful jerk. Mick's world turned white with a pain like lightning and his skin started with sweat as his arm slid back into its socket. The relief was as sudden as the pain had been, and reverberated through his body like a roll of thunder signaling the end, but of what he was not sure.

Post Mortem

The Common Room was cool and quiet, a refuge from the turmoil and turbulence of the past hours. Even better, it was real, not a scene of shreds and patches but a solid, substantial setting into which they settled like grateful pilgrims after a long journey. Kath spoke first in answer to a question Mick hadn't asked.

"I honestly don't know Mick. It's hard to remember. I don't have any idea how I came to be here. I don't remember very much between you closing the bedroom door and me getting off the coach in front of the hotel. Things come back in flashes, separate scenes like snapshots in an album, but with huge blank spaces in between."

"Let it go, Kath. You don't need to. remember."

"Yes I do need. I need to figure out what was going on, because I feel like a lot of it happened when I wasn't looking. Bear with me? The next thing I remember after getting off the bus is talking with Greenie, and then having a bath and falling asleep. And that leads to another huge blank while I was sleeping, with nothing in it except for a feeling of terrible fear, that something very very bad was hovering, waiting to get me. I can remember that feeling, and it was awful, but I can't remember what I was afraid of."

"I've had dreams like that, where there's nothing but feeling, no action. They can be very disturbing. Especially if the feeling is still there when you wake up."

"This one was disturbing, all right, but I don't remember waking up, or how I got from the Inn to the headland. The next snapshot is a meadow, and I'm talking to Tiernon, who is standing on the sea. I remember the words we were saying, but there was no sound, like a silent movie. Or a dream. So it must have been

333

a dream. He reaches out to me, and I reach to take his hand and then the next minute I'm hanging in thin air and looking down at waves crashing and foaming so far below me. And there's nothing but air in between, and I know I am going to fall."

"Oh no, you aren't. I'm in between. I'm holding you."

"I didn't know that. I didn't know what stopped my fall. And I was scared to death. Facing death."

"Small wonder," said Mick.

"And then I could feel something holding me, and I didn't know it was you, but I knew it was real. I was scraping and banging against the rocks, and I could hear the waves crash, and I could smell the sea. If I'd been dreaming before, I knew for sure I was awake then. And I'm awake now, and I know I wouldn't be here this minute if it weren't for you. I'd be down in the Sea-King's palace with fifty feet of cold green water between me and the rest of my life. I do know that much. Oh, Mick . . ."

She floundered to a stop, looking so fragile and lovely and lost that he wanted to gather her in his arms and keep her safe forever.

But with his shoulder so recently pulled from its socket that would have been awkward, so he settled instead for the light approach.

"I guess it takes hanging by a thread — literally — to make you appreciate my finer qualities. It's a good thing you've lost weight, or I'd probably have dropped you. But I think that dress is ready for the rag-bag."

"I appreciate your finer qualities, all right. So the hanging thread served its purpose." She tried a grin, but so shaky and lopsided he saw she was on the verge of tears.

"So was hanging in midair another snapshot?"

"Yes. And no. It was different. We'd been dancing, I remember that. We were all in a line winding around and in, and I knew it was the maze, and I was going to the center to meet . . . someone. And then, zip! I was out over thin air and the dance was over, and all of a sudden I didn't know who I was or why. Like going with no transition from a lovely dream to a weird nightmare. You know how things happen in dreams."

"I know how they happen. But I also know it's all right now, and I want you to know it too. The nightmare's over. You're all right now."

"No I'm not. There's something I have to tell you. When I said I was scared I didn't mean scared of falling, I meant scared of wanting to fall. Like that time I told you about with the Billy Goats Gruff, remember? That's what was so terrifying. Ever since we first came up here, I think I've been wanting to fall. And that frightens me more than anything. There've been times this past year when I wondered if I wasn't well and truly round the bend."

Me too, he thought, but did not say so. "Don't be silly. You're not round the bend. You're with me. Everything's all right."

"Well, no it isn't, not exactly. Everything's not exactly all right."

He had forgotten her stubborn streak. She went on.

"First of all, because you're not all right. Your arm's still in bad shape, and we'll have to get it seen to as soon as we get back to town. Second, because I still don't understand why these things were happening. I mean, why it was me. This was no story. This was real."

"Real enough." Unexpected, uninvited, Tiernon walked into the common room and into the conversation. He pulled out a chair, sat down, and joined the debate. "But because it was real doesn't mean it wasn't also part of the Story. And besides," he told them, "you survived, the both of you. We all survived. So that's that. It's over for another year."

Mick stared at him drop-jawed, feeling the anger build hot and hard inside him. "Is that all you have to say? That it's over and we survived? So now we all live happily ever after, or until next year, whichever comes first? Is that the idea?"

"Easy, boyo. It's not a bad idea, when you think about it. Saves a power of trouble in the long run. No hard feelings, eh?"

"What's all this talk about feelings?" said Greenie, backing through the swing door with a laden tray in her hands. "Looks to me like there's been enough feeling for one day. The Story's over for this year, everyone's well out of it, and now we could all use a nice sit-down." She thumped the tray down on the table. "I thought we might be in need of a snack after all that excitement. Something to tide us over. Dinner's in the oven, but it won't be on the table for another couple of hours."

Half risen from his seat, Mick was about to unleash his anger and let Greenie have it, when he felt Kath kick him under the table, saw her barely perceptible shake of the head, saw her lips form a silent *please*. Their glances locked, he nodded, and sank back.

Whatever it takes to get her out of here in one piece, he thought.

Greenie's snack was tempting. There was half a loaf of bread, brown and crusty, with a pot of salty yellow butter beside it. There was a bowl of winter pears from the cellar, flanked by a large golden wedge of cheese with moisture beading like pearls on its surface. There was a pitcher of dark brown cider, cool and bubbly, and four glasses ready to be filled. He realized how hungry he was.

"Eat up," said Greenie. "It's slack time and the bar's empty. And I'm thinking we'll have few customers tonight."

With his free hand Tiernon filled the glasses and handed them round.

"Drink up," he said, and raised his glass in salute.

"Cheers all round," said Greenie.

Time Out

Late that night, Mick and Kath were two solitary figures in the empty room. Dinner had been got through with no casualties; Greenie and Tiernon in the kitchen were doing the washing-up, their voices a murmur in the splash of water and the clatter of dishware and cutlery.

Mick was first to speak. "Tired?" *Stupid question*, he thought. *Of course she's tired. How not?*

She shrugged, half smiled. "I guess so. Beyond tired, I think, wherever that is. I just feel blank. Emptied. Out of gas."

"What do you want to do now?"

"I don't know. What do you want?"

"I know what I don't want. I don't want to hang around here any longer. I want to get the hell out, leave it all behind."

"Feels to me like it's left us behind."

"How do you mean?"

She picked at a splinter in the table edge, looked down at her fingers, looked up at Mick. "Oh, you know, like a theatre after the show is over and everybody's gone home. That sort of dead, dusty feeling, you know? The house lights come up and the cleaning people come in and start turning up the seats and picking up the trash. One more performance gone into thin air." She tried to smile, but stuck halfway.

He looked at her carefully. She was still in shock, but that was to be expected after everything that had happened. Eyes unnaturally bright, smile pasted on. At the same time she looked wrung out, with dark smudges under her eyes. "You've got the right word, I think: performance. The show must go on. But we don't have to."

"I guess we don't. We've said all there is to say. To them, at least."

"So how about it, Kath? We could leave tonight. Right now. I can make it happen. Just say the word."

"Mick, you shouldn't be driving. In case you've forgotten, you have a bum arm. And I honestly don't think I can face that long drive after a day as weird and exhausting as this one has been. I'm played out."

"I can face the drive, arm and all. My other arm's fine, and I'll be careful going around corners. I'm pretty sure your played-out condition will improve once we've really left the show behind. All you have to do is keep me company. I want us to go home."

He paused. She was listening. Was she with him or not? She said nothing, so he went on, searching for words to fill the silence, to give her time.

"Look, Kath, I want to get us the hell and gone away from these people. They're living in two different worlds, and it's the other one that's real for them, not the one you and I live in, that I want us to live in. They all buy into the same dream. Or the same performance, if you like. And then they come back to everyday — whatever that is — and life goes on until the next time."

341

"What else can it do? Life always goes on, doesn't it? People keep going. They remember things. They tell stories."

"Life and art don't always imitate each other. Sometimes art goes out on a limb. But we don't have to go with it."

"Don't we? I'm not so sure. Do you still think—could you really think after today—that it's all just art? Just stories? I think for people like Greenie and Tiernon—and Elly—art is life. The world is made of stories. I've learned that much at least."

"Okay. For the sake of argument, okay. But if it is, then let's for god's sake make our own story and live in our own world. I don't belong in theirs, and I don't believe you do either. But I don't know what you want."

He hesitated, waiting for a sign. She said nothing, so he went on.

"I know what I want. I want to go home."

She was on the edge of something. Tears? Anger? He couldn't tell. He waited for her to speak, for the axe to fall, for his world to end.

She took a deep breath, let it out. "I want to go home too."

Mick felt his heart turn over.

"Can we go home, Mick? The two of us?"

"Sure we can," he said. "I'll get the car."

He was getting up to leave when the kitchen door swung open and through it came Tiernon.

"You caught us just as we were leaving," said Mick.

"Heading up to bed are you?" asked Tiernon. "Can't say I blame you. It's been a long day. And an eventful one. You'll be needing your sleep. Get rested up for the drive home. I suppose you'll be leaving tomorrow?"

"No, we're leaving tonight," Mick told him. "Now, as a matter of fact."

"At this hour? Don't be daft. It's getting on for midnight."

"Doesn't matter. Kath really wants to go home, and I need to get this arm properly seen to. The sooner we're on the road, the better we'll both be."

Tiernon stared at him. "That's not a good idea, boyo. You can't drive safely with an injured arm. Besides, the road's dark as pitch and the moon won't be up till late. Go zooming around one of those hairpin turns, you'll wind up in the sea. Better stay the night here, what's left of it, and get an early start tomorrow."

"Not tomorrow. Tonight," Mick said stubbornly.

Tiernon tried again. "There's a story on the news that a nasty squall is making up offshore. Moving this way pretty fast. Storms this time of year can be bad. You don't want to be out in the middle of one."

"All the more reason for us to get a head start. We'll outrun it, be gone before it comes ashore."

Tiernon gave Mick a long look, shrugged, started to speak, thought better of it and turned to leave, then hesitated and turned back. "Look, it's none of my business, not anymore, but I'll tell you what I think straight out, and I'm serious now. Don't push the luck, boyo. Wasn't today enough for you? Don't try it again. It's time now for you to leave well enough alone, play it safe. I wouldn't take unnecessary risk if I were you."

But you're not me, thought Mick defiantly. *And I'm not you. Not by a long shot. Unecessary's all in how you see it. I am taking Kath away from here just as fast as I can. I am taking her home.* "I said we're going, and that's that," he said shortly. "Thanks for your hospitality." He

344

hoped the jab hit home, but did not stay to see its effect.

✦ ✦ ✦

Standing in the lighted doorway waving goodbye, Greenie and Tiernon watched the tail-lights recede as the car carrying Mick and Kath pulled out of the car-park, turned the corner and disappeared out of sight.

"She's not done yet," said Greenie.

"No more is he," said Tiernon. "They've a long road ahead."

"I hate to see them go," said Greenie.

A random leaf blew past, borne on a wind from the sea.

"They'll be back," said the Grally Tusker.

Spiderweb Alley

Mick let out a sigh of mingled relief and exasperation. He shifted into high gear, eased his bad arm against the back of the seat. "Goodbye to The Wicken Tree, and good riddance."

"I'd rather say, goodbye and God bless," said Kath. "But Mick, you were right. I'm glad to be gone. To be out of it and going home, safe and sound, and with you."

He smiled but did not reply. They drove in silence for a while. The weather was worsening, the offshore wind bringing bursts of rain that clattered on the car roof like hail. Tiernon's future prediction looked like it was becoming a present reality. The wind roared through the treetops, blending with the sound of waves coming in and coming in. The rain washed across the windscreen in sheets.

Mick broke the silence. "I hate to say it, but looks like Tiernon was right about that storm. We're going into it, not away from it. I doubt we'll be able to get out from under. What do you say? We can stop and wait it out, or try to weather it."

"Let's weather it, but not too fast, Mick. We don't want Tiernon to be right about us winding up in a ditch."

The wind was gaining strength now, its gale force lashing the trees into fury. Mick slowed the car, trying to hold a steady pace.

"Cold, Kath? Want my jacket?"

"No, I'm all right. I've got my sweater. It's not really cold. Just the wind."

A violent gust blew across the road driving the rain—and the car—sideways, and Mick had to fight to keep on course.

"Mick, look out!"

There was a thump against the front bumper. Mick jammed on the brakes and spun the wheel, swerving the car off onto the shoulder where it came to a bone-jolting stop, nose down in a ditch.

"We hit something."

"Felt like it. I'll have a look." He got out and surveyed the road. "Nothing there."

A yelp came from the side of the road.

Kath opened her door and slid out. "Look there, in the underbrush. It's a dog! We must have hit it."

Cowering in the ditch, just beyond the headlights, was a huddled shape.

"Kath, it's pouring buckets. Get back in the car, and I'll get us out of this."

Ignoring the order, she crouched down and reached a hand, touching gently for injury while Mick stood impatient by the car.

"Better be careful. If it's hurt it might snap at you."

"I'll be careful."

The dog, a red and white terrier, quieted under her hands. A tail wagged feebly.

Feeling over the little body as softly as she could, she reported. "I think he's not hurt, just shocked and scared." Carefully, cautiously, she slid her hands under the tense, quivering body, picking it up and cradling it gently. The dog endured her touch.

"I wonder where he came from, why he's out in this storm."

"Will you please get in the car? You're soaking wet, and so am I, and I don't relish just standing around."

"You know what, Mick? I think it's that same little dog. The one I saw the first time we were here. Remember? The red and white."

"That was ages ago. I doubt it's the same one."

"I'm sure it is. Poor little thing. And how strange, that we nearly hit him a year ago, and now we did. Maybe it's an omen, telling us we're done here, that it's time to go."

Grabbing her elbow he raised her to her feet, started her toward the car. "The dog's not hurt. He'll be okay."

"But Mick, we can't just leave him after we've hit him." She was walking to the car as she spoke, the dog cradled protectively in her arms.

"Yes we can."

"Can't we take him with us? Look how thin he is. He's a stray. He's got tag, no collar, and his ribs are sticking out. He's nobody's pet." Sliding into the passenger seat, she cradled the

349

dog on her lap, took off her sweater and covered him with it.

"What exactly do you plan to do with nobody's pet?"

"Don't be angry, Mick, please don't be angry."

"I'm not angry, I just want to know what you're going to do."

"I don't know what I'm going to do. This isn't something I planned. He's nobody's dog. He could be ours." She bent over the dog.

He licked her ear.

"We don't need a dog, certainly not a stray loaded with fleas and lord knows what-all."

"He needs us."

"What you mean is, you need him."

No reply.

"Okay. I surrender. If this is what it takes to get you home, so be it. We've got a dog. Now can we go?" He started the car, backed cautiously out of the ditch and onto the road, and took off into the storm with a screech of rubber on the wet roadway.

They navigated in silence for a while, Mick with his eyes stubbornly on the road, Kath with her eyes on Mick and her hands on the dog, stroking, soothing, calming his shivers.

"Selkie, hmmm? We'll call him Selkie."

"That's no name for a dog."

"Well, I just thought . . . but not if you don't like it."

"I honestly don't care. Call him anything you like."

"Thank you, Mick."

The rain clattered against the windshield like thrown gravel, drowning any possibility of conversation. The wind was a steady roar, lashing the rain and bending the trees sideways till they flung their arms like demented clowns in a pantomime. The road was strewn with leaves and twigs and fallen branches, some of them sizeable ones that had to be navigated around, so that Mick was forced to drive at a crawl for much of the time.

Gradually there came a change, at first felt more than seen. The wind was more fitful, coming in gusts rather than the steady hurricane it had been. The clouds were still lowering, still black, but behind the clouds the sky was a shade less dark, barely beginning to lighten toward a dawn still too far off to see. The road dipped, swinging closer to the shore, and ran into a hollow that gave some shelter from the storm. They got glimpses of steep shingle and, beyond that, barely visible wet rocks looming like troll statues, and, in and around the rocks, the black sea swirling and sucking, heaving like a live thing, so close to the car they could almost feel the waves pounding.

Mick, listening, slowed the car. "What's that knocking?"

"I don't hear anything. Couldn't, with this wind."

"Sounded like something underneath the car, scraping and banging. Something lodged in the undercarriage."

"Maybe one of those fallen branches. Might have knocked the tailpipe loose?"

"I'll have a look." He pulled off, dangerously close to where the land slanted down to the sea edge, braked, got out and went round the back to have a look. What happened then occurred so quickly and in such rapid sequence that at the time he could not keep up with it, though afterward he could remember every moment, etched on his memory as clear as glass.

Kath opened her door to get out, and as she did the dog sprang off her lap and took off running seaward.

"Hey!" she shouted, and without thought or hesitation slid out of her seat and ran in pursuit of the little dark shape scampering, barely visible among the darker rocks, her discarded sweater dropped by the roadside. *He's so scared he doesn't know where he's going*, she thought.

He was running straight toward the incoming seas crashing and spilling on the shingle.

Oblivious to the rising water, Kath stumbled, caught her balance, went on.

Soaked to the skin and crouching down to check the tailpipe, Mick heard her shout and glanced up in time to see her moving shape against the moving water.

"Kath! You crazy woman! Come back here! Where do you think you're going?"

She was out in the surf now, knee deep amid the suck and swirl of the waves that dragged at her skirts, threading the half-submerged rocks in pursuit of the sleek wet head just above the water even farther out.

He was paddling furiously to keep afloat, riding the undertow and moving farther and farther away from her after every surge.

"Kath come back here! Get away from those rocks!"

A rogue wave caught Kath broadside, knocking her under and pulling her inexorably into the undertow. She disappeared and then her head broke the surface yards out. She was swimming furiously, fighting the water to get to her desire.

"I'm coming!" she cried. "Wait for me!"

Mick heard a high sharp yip, like a seal's bark. He started running. "Kath! You'll never get him! Give it up! Let him go!"

Waves were coming faster, and far out Mick could make out lines of white foam where the breakers were rolling in and rolling in, tops cresting and falling like mountains rushing to take the shore, the water crashing and swirling, deliberate and pitiless as fate. One tall buttress of rock, an extension of the cliff, reached far out into the water. It was hollowed, the center eaten away by wind and water into a natural gateway like the letter n, around and through which the water boiled and surged. Out beyond the others one huge wave was mounting impossibly high, topping, curling, crashing though the opening to fall onto the shore like thunder, like doom.

Kath was fighting the element.

Without hesitation, Mick plunged after her, but a surge of water greater than his strength could resist sent him back against the rocks. He could barely see Kath's shape as the water hurled her through the gateway to follow the furiously swimming beast-shape cradled in the wave that mounded and crested and toppled and fell in on her.

Mick saw the sea's arms wrap around Kath, saw her sink into the embrace that pulled her under to where she had always been going. And then she was gone.

The next wave incoming slammed into Mick and knocked him sideways off his feet, and his head struck a rock, and the world dissolved into foam and chaos as the sea took him too, and rolled him up onto the shingle, random and helpless as a piece of driftwood.

✦ ✦ ✦

Time folded around him as he woke vomiting seawater in gushes that dragged his lungs up into his throat.

"That's the ticket," said a voice somewhere near him. "Up and out."

Mick vomited again, a bitter slosh of seawater and grit and sour bile that surged like floodtide into his mouth. Emptied at last, he dragged air into his lungs, air that burned like fire and made a sound like cloth tearing. He coughed, spat, coughed again. His mouth felt swollen, and he tasted blood. He lay on wet shingle, soaked and battered while the world gradually took shape in his blurred vision.

"Here, I'll help you up," said Tiernon.

He struggled to stand, and the world rocked under his feet.

"Can you walk? Better let me take your arm. And look out for those rocks. We get shipwrecks, you know, in the storm season."

The rain was lessening, coming in gusts rather than torrents as the gale blew itself out, the wind sweeping the new sky clean of clouds, making room for the sun. A line of light ran like molten silver along the horizon, dividing sea from sky.

It was going to be a fine day.

— Mia Palladino, 2024

For the curious, here's a sneak peek at

Book Two
of
THE ELVERIE ROAD

The Wicken Tree

Typical late autumn weather poured buckets, and Mick drove all that day through a dim grey landscape to the rhythmic *swish-thump* of the windshield wipers and the hiss of tires on wet pavement. Toward late afternoon the downpour subsided and the cloud cover began to break up. As sometimes happens after a storm, the changing light changed everything. The setting sun broke through a rift in the cloud,

The setting sun broke through a rift in the cloud, dyeing the air rose gold, setting fire to the hilltops and burnishing the whitecaps far out to sea. Creating a different world.

At the Scenic Route exit Mick swung the car off the motorway and immediately cut his speed by half. Already tired from the day's drive, he remembered that the route was not just scenic, it was hair-raising, a narrow ribbon twisting along sheer hillsides with rocky hillsides on one side and a tree-bordered cliff with a straight drop to the sea on the other. Tricky to drive when dry, it was treacherous when, as now, it was slick with rain. The hairpin turns were too easy to overshoot, and before you knew it you'd be diving fifty or so feet straight down — destination: ocean.

What was it Kath had said?

"This road is an accident waiting to happen."

Too right it was, and not the only one.

"You, Kath. You were an accident waiting to happen."

And then the wait had ended, and the accident had happened. And now all he had left of her was this conversation in his head, a perpetual replay between past and present where he allowed himself to say all the things he'd never said.

You can't win an argument with a dead woman, he told himself. *Forget about it. It's a losing game. She's been gone — how long? Not even a year but it seems like forever. Seems like yesterday. And we are still bickering. Maybe we always will be.*

It was better than nothing, though, and it was all he had of her now. So he went on arguing.

So did she.

How many twists and turns does this road have, anyway?

"As many as you had, and that was too many for me."

Can't we go a little farther?

"How far did you want to go?"

Even as the questions replayed themselves — probably because *they* did — his gaze was pulled inevitably to the tall rock arch looming offshore.

As far as she went. The Sea Gate and Kath's final destination.

He couldn't look away from the angry waves that boiled and battered through the arch, fountaining up its height before falling back to be sucked inexorably into the undertow of the next wave. As Kath had been.

Wrenching his gaze back to the road, Mick rejoined the argument.

Kath: *I'll be all right. I have to do this.*

Mick: "The hell you did. Nobody made you. And you were anything but all right."

Kath: *Please please please understand.*

Mick: "No way. I didn't understand then, and I don't now. Dammit, Kath, why can't you be like other people?"

Stupid question. She wasn't like other people. She was Kath. She was herself. A free spirit if ever there was one. The poem he'd told as a joke now sent chills up his spine:

> *Up the airy mountain,*
> *Down the rushy glen,*
> *We daren't go a-hunting*
> *For fear of little men.*
> *They stole little Bridget*
> *For seven years long;*
> *When she came down again*
> *Her friends were all gone.*

And she had said, chillingly, "Seven years might be worth a human lifetime."

That's my girl, he thought. *Until you changed your mind. Until you told me, "I don't want to be Little Bridget any more." Until you said the words I was waiting to hear: "I want to go home."*

They still had the power to wring his heart.

"I wanted to take you home, Kath. Heaven knows I tried. But by that time it was too late."

He kept the argument going, because it was the only way he could be with her now.

"Little Bridget came back after seven years," he told her. "But you got yourself a one-way ticket." He caught his own eyes in the rearview mirror. "And you?" he asked himself. "What are you a-hunting? And why?"

He thought he knew. He was following his nose and the yellow brick road all the way there and back again to find someone who could tell him what it meant, that Kath had done what she did. He could feel the anger building cold and hard in his midriff, its icy weight, like a snowball with a stone inside, pressing him forward. The sun was gone now, drowned in the ocean while the horizon was still glorious and at the zenith the first stars were starting to appear. He glanced at his watch, at the sky, then at the road.

Nearly there.

The snowball was pressing harder now. Pressing back, he jammed his foot on the gas pedal, took a blind corner on two wheels and overshot the turnoff to the Inn by fifty feet. He slammed on the brake, jerked into high speed reverse, fishhooked backwards into the driveway, did a three-point turn into the car park, killed the engine, got out, and slammed the car door so hard the window rattled. Announcing his arrival, if anyone was listening. Of course no one was.

The lantern above the door shone down on the hanging signboard announcing: THE WICKEN TREE — INN AND PUBLIC HOUSE. The sign swung gently, creaking a little in the wind. The place looked much the same. The weatherworn fieldstone walls of the Inn bulged at the corners and the window-frames sagged like eyes that had seen too much. The well with its bucket on a hook still sat next to the flat stump, all that was left of the tree that must once have shaded the doorstep.

Behind the windows of the common room figures moved like puppets in a theatre.

His gaze moved up to the dormer of little attic room he remembered, tucked high under the rooftree. That window was blank. His eyes blurred and the outlines wavered, almost disappearing. Road fatigue.

All right then. Here we go.

He took a deep breath and mounted the shallow stone steps. The front door was unlatched, and he pushed it open and went in.

✦ ✦ ✦

Book Two
of
THE ELVERIE ROAD

The Wicken Tree

by
Verlyn Flieger

is in production and will be published
in the near future by The Gabbro Head.

About the Author

Verlyn Flieger is Professor Emerita in the Department of English at the University of Maryland, where for 36 years she taught courses in J. R. R. Tolkien, medieval literature, and comparative mythology. Currently, she is Editor Emerita for *Tolkien Studies*, a yearly journal devoted to the work of J. R. R. Tolkien.